Gillian Avery

Born in Surrey, England, GILLIAN AVERY began her career as a newspaper reporter and worked for some years as a staff member of *Chambers Encyclopaedia* and the Oxford University Press. When she and her husband, A.O.J. Cockshut, moved to Manchester, Avery began to write a cycle of novels set in Oxford in the 1870s. She drew largely on her interest in Victorian children's fiction to create this cycle, which includes *The Warden's Niece*, *Trespassers at Charlecote*, *James Without Thomas*, *The Peacock House*, and *The Elephant War*. Among Avery's later works are a series of six books for younger readers and two full-length historical novels, *Call of the Valley* and *A Likely Lad*, which won the Guardian award for children's fiction in 1971.

As well as being a prolific writer, Gillian Avery is an authority on historical children's books. She is currently engaged in completing a history of American children's books. *The Oxford Companion to Children's Literature* credits Avery's *The Warden's Niece*, published in 1957, as "one of the children's books that marked the beginning of a renaissance in English juvenile fiction."

YEARLING CLASSICS

Works of lasting literary merit by English
and American classic and contemporary writers

YEARLING BOOKS / YOUNG YEARLINGS / YEARLING CLASSICS
are designed especially to entertain and enlighten young people.
Charles F. Reasoner, Professor Emeritus of Children's Literature
and Reading, New York University, is consultant to this series.

For a complete listing of all Yearling titles, write to
Dell Readers Service, P.O. Box 1045,
South Holland, IL 60473.

The Elephant War

Gillian Avery

With an Afterword by Jean Fritz

Published by
Dell Publishing
a division of
The Bantam Doubleday Dell Publishing Group, Inc.
1 Dag Hammarskjold Plaza
New York, New York 10017

NOTE

The sale of Jumbo to Barnum's Circus and the frenzy that it caused in England did not in fact take place until 1882. I have transplanted the bare facts of the sale to 1875, and have invented a wholly fictitious reaction to it by the people of Oxford; the only details which have any historical accuracy are the two telegrams sent by the *Daily Telegraph* and by Barnum, and the quotations from "Jumbo's March."

The verse sung by the Smith boys on page 86 is taken from George Barker: *Two Plays*, published in 1958 by Messrs. Faber & Faber, and I am grateful for their permission to use it.

This work was first published in Great Britain by William Collins Ltd. 1960 and by The Bodley Head Ltd. 1985

Yearling ® TM 913705, Dell Publishing,
a division of The Bantam Doubleday Dell Publishing Group, Inc.

ISBN: 0-440-40040-6

RL: 6.1

Printed in the United States of America

First U.S.A. Printing
March 1988

10 9 8 7 6 5 4 3 2 1

W

Contents

The Elephant War

Chapter 1

Three Boys

*H*arriet first saw the Smiths in the Ashmolean Museum on a bleak February day in 1875. There they were, three of them, all boys, clustered around a glass case which held a violin, and talking loudly and confidently as they peered in. There was a tall, thin, black-haired one who was lounging rather languidly, a smaller, brown one of eleven or so, Harriet's own age, and a plump red-headed child with a dogged expression; he was standing on tiptoe, and had his face so near the glass that his breath was making clouds on it. One way and another they were attracting a good deal of attention. So far as Harriet herself was concerned, she immediately forgot about the newspaper placards in the street outside, which said "Beloved Elephant. London Zoo Tragedy." She stopped questioning Miss Edale about what it could possibly mean, and stood still, looking at them. Miss Edale, a large, mild-mannered lady, who had no more idea what the placards meant than Harriet, paused thankfully by a carved oak armchair, looked around a little nervously, and then sank into it. Harriet hesitated for a moment, then with an air of being passionately interested in Greek coins, she walked over to the showcase next to the one that held the violin, and stared in fixedly.

"I think it's terribly sad," the middle boy was saying earnestly. "The violin lying here all these years, just boxed up and silent. It's like burying someone alive."

"Don't be so sentimental, Joshua," said the biggest boy lazily. "You're anthropomorphizing—you know you are." (But he pronounced the word rather hesitatingly, as though he were hardly sure how many syllables it had.)

The plump red-headed boy lifted his head for a moment. "Yes, that's right, he is. Making it human. Papa said he was anthro—whatever it is when he felt sorry for the hot-water tank because as soon as it filled itself up somebody emptied it again. Joshua could feel sorry for anything," he added contemptuously.

"Well, look at it," Joshua said wistfully. "Its strings all broken too. I wonder if the person who played on it knew it was the last time that it would ever sound. Perhaps he was dying and ripped them so that nobody else could play. Or perhaps he was so dissatisfied with his own playing that he tore them in despair."

"More likely he hurled it at another musician in a fit of temper," said the tall boy. "You know what these Italians are, full of fire and fury." He poked at the red-headed boy. "James, take your nose off that glass; you'll go through it."

Harriet was enthralled. She thought it was the most witty, intelligent conversation she had ever heard, just the sort of thing that she had hoped of Oxford. She had imagined that the move to Oxford, three months ago, from the dark, damp town in the north Midlands where her father had practiced as a doctor would be the turning point in her life. She had pored over the battered book of engravings of Oxford, trying to build up a picture of it in her mind before she arrived. She was not disappointed as they drove up from the station. It was all so gray and old, and at every corner a fresh tower or spire came into sight. But the station hansom presently left all this behind. Great-Uncle Harry, whose practice Dr. Jessop had now inherited, had moved just before he died to a new house on the outskirts of Oxford, and it was to this bleak and rather ugly suburb that Harriet and her parents came to live. The house was tall and thin, built of fierce red brick, with elaborate battlements over the porch, as though it were trying to look like old Oxford. But it did not in the least, Harriet thought. In fact, she preferred their old house in the dark industrial town they had come from. There at least the soot that clung to the bricks gave a certain age to the building. Worst of all about this one was the way that the houses on either side pressed in, so that when you were in the small pinched garden you were surrounded by them, with blank windows like eyes peering down.

They sent her to the Oxford Ladies' College because her mother wanted her to be really well educated, and this was one of the new schools that gave girls the same sort of education that boys received. Her mother was a great admirer of Miss Raby, the Lady Principal, but Harriet, as she struggled with Euclid and algebra and Latin, wished that nobody had ever thought of improving girls' education. She was in one of the lowest forms, with girls mostly younger than herself, and nobody paid her much attention, or talked to her. Before school and after it she hung about near the school gates wondering whether the older girls who stood in groups brightly chattering were the professors' daughters that her father had promised she should meet.

Not that she ever had very long to wait. Her mother, brisk and efficient as always, had engaged Miss Edale to look after her out of school hours and during vacations, for she herself was far too busy with her charitable works. So Miss Edale met her when school finished, and Miss Edale took her for walks. She was mild and kind, the daughter of a clergyman Mrs. Jessop had once known, but she had nothing to say to Harriet, and Harriet had nothing to say to her. It was when Harriet was with Miss Edale that her disappointment about Oxford became keenest. There was Miss Edale, with a father who had been at the University, and yet she knew nothing about it at all. For Harriet's benefit she stumblingly tried to remember which college was which, but she contradicted herself and changed her mind so often that the only one that Harriet was certain of was Christ Church because Miss Edale sometimes used to attend services at the cathedral there. So the walks that they took through the winding, narrow streets of the University became a torment rather than a pleasure because of the feeling of being outside it all. What was the use of peering up at these beauties, minarets and spires and ancient stonework, if there was nobody to tell you what they were. Harriet felt lonely, outside the laughter and the chatter of the passing young men, the lamplight that came from uncurtained windows in the narrow lanes between colleges in the dark winter afternoons. Fortunately, perhaps, they never lingered in these streets where Harriet tormented herself. Miss Edale only liked walks with a purpose, the Botanical Gardens, or the University Parks, and seemed surprised in her mild way if Harriet wanted to stop and look at something. So they plodded silently down the same roads every day, never varying the side of the street, only breaking their routine if it was wet, when they went to the Ashmolean. Harriet used to look at gay groups of children, wondering how they knew each other, and whether their fathers belonged to the University. Sometimes she even furtively tried to quicken the pace of the walk so that they could catch up with the children and perhaps hear what they were talking about.

To overhear today's conversation in the Ashmolean, so assured and knowledgeable, from boys who seemed to be in the habit of talking like that all day long, was one of the most exciting things that had yet happened to her in Oxford. She bent over the Greek coins and tried to look sideways at the boys through her eyelashes. But they seemed to have extracted all possible interest from the violin, and the eldest was already moving away. He was followed by the red-headed one, who remarked that he was sure it must be nearly teatime, and that Cook had promised them muffins if the muffin man passed. The last to go was the boy they had called Joshua, who pressed his face closer to the case and then sighed and followed his brothers. Harriet, giving up all pretense about Greek coins, watched them leave the room. They were probably going out of her life forever. She would never see them again. In her despair she did something bolder than she had ever done before; she walked up to one of the museum porters, who was standing sleepily by the door.

"If you please, can you tell me who those three boys were who have just gone out?" As she said it she realized it was such an extraordinary question to ask that she became hot all over, and nearly fled without waiting for the answer. But the porter gave no sign of thinking it odd. He gazed past Harriet through the door where they had disappeared. He had a straggly mustache and made a sucking noise as he talked.

"Ah. You can see *they're* not short." He paused and sucked his teeth admiringly. "They don't often come here, but they always says something very witty. Very witty. I usually tries to remember it to tell my youngsters. Now what was it today. Something about the Eyetalians?" He puzzled over it, pulling on his mustache. Harriet waited.

"Do you know who they are, please?" she ventured at last, feeling very young and very silly.

The porter looked at her in great surprise. "Oh, I don't know who they *are*. We don't hear people's names in here. We just observes their behavior," he said in a very dignified manner.

"Though, wait a bit. Their pa did come in with them once, and I think I did hear one of my mates say as he was a professor. But of course I couldn't say for certain. Ah, they're not short, those young gentlemen, not they." He shook his head, and seemed to go off into a dream. Harriet crept away and joined Miss Edale.

Miss Edale was regarding something on the wall with deep attention, and had apparently not observed Harriet's conversation with the porter. She seemed to be strangely excited, though all Harriet could see was a piece of rather yellowed lace in a small glass case. " 'Thought to be the longest piece of Venetian rose-point lace made in England,' " she read out from the label. " 'Ten yards.' "

"It doesn't seem very much," said Harriet after a pause, her mind still on the boys as she wondered what sort of clever remark they would be able to make about lace.

"But Harriet, the labor! Just look at the intricacy of the pattern—like carved ivory. Now, do you know what I am thinking? I myself embarked on some rose-point lace when I was a girl, and I completed twelve inches, I think. If I were to work at it really hard I might very well be able to make a piece longer than the one in this museum. Now is that not a splendid target to set oneself? My dear father always used to tell us children to bide our time and the Lord would provide an opportunity for each of us to distinguish himself at something. What a very fine thing it would be. Dear me, I can hardly wait to begin afresh.

It hardly seemed the moment to question Miss Edale about the three boys, and, besides, if she did not even know the names of the colleges she would hardly know the names of the professors' children. However, although it was such a forlorn hope, Harriet was so eager to know about them that as soon as Miss Edale had ceased talking of the lace she brought up the subject. One never knew, perhaps by some marvelous chance she would be a friend of the family, and offer to introduce Harriet.

But it appeared that she had not even noticed them. "You think they were a professor's children? No, I am afraid I have not the least notion who they could be. Now, if only I had a good head for figures I could work out how long I should have to devote myself to my lace in order to complete, say, eleven yards. I think I can spare three hours a day. Harriet, I am sure they make you do mental arithmetic at your school—perhaps you can work out the sum."

Harriet struggled with it, and became so preoccupied with wrestling over the figures that she fell off the curb twice. "I think it will be sixty-three years," she said at last.

Miss Edale was very downcast. "Dear me, that will mean I will be a hundred and four, and I cannot hope with any confidence that it will be given to me to live so long, though a great-aunt of mine did live to be ninety-two. Harriet, I feel sure we must have made a mistake in our reckoning somewhere. After all, it did not take me so very long to do those twelve inches when I was a girl, and I intend to devote much more of my time to it now.

But Harriet's brain felt bruised by the effort it had made to work out the sum, and she could not attempt any more. Besides, her heart was not really in it. She was wondering what the boys were talking about over their muffins, and whether by any chance they had noticed her studying the Greek coins.

In the Jessops' drawing room on Bradmore Road her parents were having tea. Dr. Jessop lay sprawled in his huge leather armchair, drinking his tea from the enormous pint-sized cup with its shelf on which to rest his mustache. Mrs. Jessop made no secret of the dislike she felt for this cup, but her husband said that those silly little eggshells designed for a race of midgets during a water shortage in the Sahara would drive any thirsty man mad, and the only concession he made was to drink his tea from one of them when there were lady visitors. Mrs. Jessop, with a frown of concentration on her face, sat on the edge of an upright chair reading a sheaf of papers. As Harriet came in she pursed her lips and shook her head slightly as she underlined something heavily and wrote a comment in the margin. Fairy, Dr. Jessop's enormous Dalmatian dog, was the first to notice. She got up from the hearth rug and lolloped over, and with clumsy affection tried to put her paws on Harriet's shoulders. Harriet tried to push her down, and at that Dr. Jessop turned his head.

"Come, come, Hetty," he said as he had said so often before. "Love me, love my dog, you know. Look at Fairy—look how pleased she is to see you. There now, good dog, you gave her a grand welcome, didn't you, and not an atom of notice did she take. Not an atom. Well, Hetty, my lass, have you seen what the *Oxford Mail* has to say about Jumbo? The elephant friend of all England's children, it calls him."

Two hours ago Harriet would indeed have wanted to know; two hours ago she had been pestering Miss Edale about the newspaper placards on the very same subject. But so excited was she about the boys that nothing else could interest her, and she brushed aside her father's remark as though she had not heard it. "Papa, do you visit any professors?" she burst out.

"Professors . . . well now, let me see. There's old Professor Tomkins of Brasenose College who's dying from the effects of seventy years of overeating. Will he suit you?"

"William," said Mrs. Jessop reprovingly, without looking up from her papers. "Harriet, your tea is in the dining room."

"But, Papa, do you know any that have children?" said Harriet desperately.

"Ha-ha, you want to move in learned circles, do you? Alice, do you hear this? Our little Hetty wants some intellectual society."

"Harriet will have to do better at school, and then she will make clever friends." Mrs. Jessop put down her papers for a moment, pushed her glasses down her nose, and looked at her. "We sent you to the right school for clever friends. Try to move out of that class of yours," she added in a kindly way. "You know that Miss Edale or I will help you with any lessons that you are finding difficult. When you are with girls of your own age you will be happier. I feel sorry you are not old enough to engage in this sort of work"—she tapped her papers with her pencil. "Then you would soon make a host of acquaintances. Now just let me finish correcting this report on the Female Prisoners' Self-Help Guild, and go away and have your tea. Then when you have done your homework you can come back here with your storybook."

Harriet ate her tea alone, shivering slightly in the cold dining room which looked out over the rather dreary road. None of the houses had been long put up, and the gardens in front of them were bare and bleak, some of them still with heaps of builders' rubble piled there, but even the gardens which had received some attention looked bleak enough, with straggling wallflower plants drooping their leaves in the damp, foggy air. Her mother came in before she had finished eating.

"Harriet, my dear, I shall have to go out after all. I must consult Mr. Abel about the drawing up of this report; it simply will not do as it stands. How inefficient people are. What, reading with your tea? What new rubbish have you this time?"

Harriet, conscious that it was rather a rubbishy book, reluctantly showed her *Miss Patty*. "A girl called Agatha in my class lent it to me," she mumbled.

Mrs. Jessop thumbed through it disapprovingly. "It's not much good wanting clever friends if that's the sort of book you read, is it? You ought to be absorbing facts, facts, facts. If you don't do it now you never will, you know. Well, I must go now if I am to catch Mr. Abel before he leaves his office."

She bustled out of the room. A moment later the front door

banged, and Harriet was left there in the cold dining room, miserably conscious that what her mother said was true. Only there were so many facts—where did one begin? How did one begin to be so clever as that family of boys with their long words and talk about Italians? She sighed, and in a hopeless way returned to *Miss Patty*, where the heroine was not only pretty and beautifully behaved, but confounded her teacher by standing up and talking French like a native. That was the sort of thing that Harriet's favorite daydreams were about.

Chapter 2

Canterbury Lane

*T*he hope that she might meet the three boys again drove every other thought out of Harriet's head, and made her almost tremble with eagerness every afternoon as she started out on her walk with Miss Edale. But it was bitter February weather, and Miss Edale suffered badly from cold hands and chilblains, and, besides, she longed to return to her lace. So although Harriet would really have liked to loiter around the part of Oxford where she had seen the boys, Miss Edale was anxious only to finish the walk as quickly as her duty to Mrs. Jessop allowed, and to return Harriet to the cold Bradmore Road dining room for her tea. If Mrs. Jessop was out, busying herself with committees (for she spared herself no day of the week except Sunday), Miss Edale would stay to have tea. This meant that Harriet had to give up all idea of reading while she ate, and licking the jam spoon at the end. And afterward, she would have to fetch her sewing. She was making, very slowly and painfully, some frocks, out of the purple merino she had outgrown last year, for the babies of the Female Prisoners.

While she sewed, Miss Edale worked at her lace. It was difficult
for both of them to get on very fast, for the dining room was
very cold and the chairs hard and too high to make sewing in
them at all comfortable. But the drawing room fire was never
lit before three o'clock, whatever the weather, for Mrs. Jessop
held that everybody should be working until that hour, and
that work kept one warm. If she was out, it was not lit at all,
and Dr. Jessop took his tea in the comfort of his study, with
Fairy noisily lapping tea and milk out of his saucer.

The Saturday after Harriet had first seen the boys, in the late
afternoon, when Harriet and Miss Edale were painfully working
by the light of the one lamp, Mrs. Jessop came in briskly
rubbing her hands.

"Dear me, Harriet," she said, "those poor babies will be
grown up with children of their own before your dresses are
ready for them, and there'll be your green merino ready for
making over at the end of this winter. How are you doing, Miss
Edale? I hope the lace progresses."

Miss Edale put down her work hastily, for she had the feeling
that Mrs. Jessop thought it a rather useless undertaking. "The
short winter afternoon makes work difficult," she said a little
nervously. "And of course during the week there are other more
important duties to devote myself to, though on Saturdays I
hope to give myself the luxury of spending all my free time on
my lace. But of course you do not spare yourself, even on
Saturdays. Was it The League of Women's Rights today?"

"It was, I am sorry to say, rather a lost afternoon," said Mrs.
Jessop, peeling off her gloves, "though the charity involved was
a worthy one. But they chose to combine the committee meeting with a tea party, and in my opinion the two should never
be mixed. The chatter! Harriet, my dear, with all your failings,
at least you do not chatter. What I would do with a chattering
daughter I really can't think."

"It is a pity to chatter over such a serious matter as Women's

Rights, perhaps," said Miss Edale. "Though I confess I enjoy a tea party myself."

"Oh it was not Women's Rights today. Professor Smith would never have permitted such a thing under his roof. He is a despot of a man," said Mrs. Jessop in her downright way. "Though if I were Mrs. Smith with such a husband and three sons I would have been driven into Women's Rights long ago."

"Three sons, Mama?" said Harriet eagerly. "Did you see them?"

"Fortunately I did not. However, Mrs. Smith talked about them at great length and spared me nothing."

"She didn't tell you their names, did she, Mama?"

"She probably did, but I was not paying very much attention at the time. I believe I recollect there was one called James, who seemed to cause her a great deal of trouble. Oh come, Harriet, this hem not finished yet! And what ugly great jags of stitches. I really think you will have to unpick them."

Harriet felt she could not question her mother any more on the subject without making her very suspicious, but a few minutes later, after she had given a lot of thought to the way she should put it, she said in a voice that she hoped was offhand: "It's a horrible cold day, Mama. We got very cold when we were out. I hope you didn't have far to go to Mrs. Smith's house." She felt almost sick with anxiety as she waited for her mother to reply. By some marvelous chance Mrs. Jessop might have met the mother of the boys. Three of them, and one called James who gave a lot of trouble—they *might* be the same ones. It would be the cruelest tragedy if her mother would not tell her where they lived. She let out her breath in a long sigh of relief as her mother replied.

"To Canterbury Lane in the middle of the town. It is, I suppose, about twenty minutes' walk, but one has only to move briskly to keep warm. I have no patience with those people who complain so incessantly about how cold they are feeling—the remedy is simple."

Harriet thought of very little else but Canterbury Lane all over the weekend, and rehearsed over and over again the way she was going to plead with Miss Edale that their walk on Monday should be in that direction, until she was in an agony, first at the thought that Miss Edale might refuse to go, and then that the Smiths might never appear at all—even supposing that they were the same boys as she had seen in the Museum.

She was so worked up by the time school ended on Monday that she ran out to Miss Edale at the gate still wrenching at the buttons on her coat and pushing her hair into her hat. "Miss Edale," she said breathlessly. "Do you know any road in Oxford called Canterbury Lane?"

"Canterbury Lane, Harriet?" Miss Edale looked very vague. "There is a Canterbury College, I know, but I am never certain which one it is. I get so confused between that and Lincoln and Exeter Colleges. Canterbury Lane—oh, but of course! That is where the needlework shop is!"

"Could we go there, do you think?"

Miss Edale became very doubtful. "The trouble is, Harriet, that last week I had a disagreement with that shop. They were very unpleasant, and I said that in the future I would have to deal with Thrupp's. I should not like them to catch sight of me near their windows and to think that I had after all changed my mind."

"But I wasn't wanting to go to the shop," Harriet said. "It was just to see the street."

"Even so, I would rather that they did not see me. Somebody might be looking out through the shop window, you know. However," said Miss Edale, weakening as she saw Harriet's anxious face, "since you are so very desirous we might just walk swiftly down the street."

And so Harriet's first objective was achieved. It was cold and raw outside, and they walked very quickly to try to keep warm. It took five minutes to get through the raw red suburbs that had sprung up to the north of Oxford, to St. Giles Church with its quiet churchyard. It was not until here that Harriet reckoned the proper Oxford began. Then there was a wide, tree-lined road with pleasant old houses, and then another church, and you were in the Oxford of the colleges and spires. It was through this part that Miss Edale walked, rather nervously looking over her shoulder as though she were afraid of being followed by a spy from the needlework shop. At length they stood at the top of a cobbled street where tall old buildings jostled each other, and the footfalls of the passing undergraduates echoed against the walls. The needlework shop was immediately recognizable, the only shop in the street. Miss Edale gave it a wary look.

"This is Canterbury Lane, Harriet. Have you seen all that you wished to see?"

Harriet gave a despairing look down the street, wondering how she could ever tell which house Professor Smith lived in. "Do you think we could walk down just a little way," she begged. "Perhaps we could see Canterbury College."

Miss Edale seemed to draw a deep breath; then she scuttled past the small window of the needlework shop with a bent head. "I am afraid I do not know which it is, unless it could be that building at the bottom with a tower over the gate. But there is no means of telling."

"There might be if we got nearer." Harriet walked very fast and hoped that Miss Edale would not argue this point. She was examining the buildings on each side of the road very anxiously. So far there did not seem to be one that could be a private house—they all seemed to be the backs of college buildings, with heavily barred windows high from the ground. But there were two at the bottom of the street that did seem to be proper houses, next to the gateway that was crowned with a tower. Both had doors painted black, and brasswork that shone, even through the gloom of the misty February afternoon.

"I don't think there really will be any notice to indicate which college it is, Harriet," said Miss Edale, hurrying after her. The road was a cul-de-sac, and she obviously felt that the needlework shop had her trapped there. But Harriet was far enough ahead to pretend politely that she had not heard this.

"I think this must be Canterbury College," she said, stopping in front of one of the black doors. "Look, here it says 'Canterbury Lodgings.' " She pointed to the highly polished brass plate on the wall.

Miss Edale peered at it. "Then this is where Warden Henniker-Hadden lives. Such a very learned man. My dear father was up at the University at the same time as he was, and was slightly acquainted with him."

But Harriet was not really listening. She was looking at the black front door of the next house. It must be there that Professor Smith lived. It must be; there was no other house on Canterbury Lane.

"Come now, Harriet," said Miss Edale. "We had better turn back now."

It was heartbreaking to go back just when she had discovered the Smiths' house. Unless they came out now she might never see them again. She lingered there forlornly, staring at the snowy-white lace that masked all that might be happening behind the windows.

"Come, Harriet," said Miss Edale once more. "We cannot stand in front of this house or the owners will be most put out."

But Harriet had heard a sound of footsteps within the house, and was unashamedly standing waiting to see whether their owners would appear. The front door swung open, and before Harriet had time to think of moving away three boys shot out, the boys she had seen at the Museum. They were closely followed by a stout, red-faced, rather jolly-looking man.

"Steady, James, steady," he said to the small red-haired boy. "There is no need to go knocking down ladies, however great your hurry. Pray excuse my son." He lifted his hat to Miss Edale, and then looked back at Harriet as she stood awkwardly there. "I am afraid our house does not merit much attention from visitors to Oxford. There is Canterbury College." He waved toward the gateway and the tower. "Or the Canterbury Lodgings here," he added, indicating the next-door house. "In fact, that footprint on the doorstep might even be the footprint of the Warden of Canterbury. Would you say so, Thomas?"

The boys were standing there behind their father, staring at Harriet. The biggest boy looked at the snowy whiteness of the step, which had a large footprint boldly imprinted in the middle.

"The warden usually goes into the Lodgings from the college side," he said in a remote way, giving Harriet rather a contemptuous look.

"Oh, dear me, so he does. Forgive me, my dear young lady, for raising false hopes. It does not look, after all, as though we can claim any distinction for the footprint." He raised his hat again, and with the boys jumping up and down on either side of him, disappeared down Canterbury Lane.

"Of course it wasn't the warden's footstep," the voice of the red-headed boy came back to them. "It was his housekeeper's. I bet you it was his housekeeper's. I know because of her galoshes with all those pimples on the bottom. Papa, weren't they her galoshes?" His voice faded into the distance.

Harriet, flushed crimson to the roots of her hair, still stood there feeling in her embarrassment and mortification quite unable to move. Miss Edale was also very put out.

"Oh dear, oh dear, oh dear," she kept saying with little gasps. "What a thing to happen. How very rude that gentleman must think we are, standing in front of his house like that so that he could hardly even get out. Come, Harriet, at once. I shall never be able to visit Canterbury Lane again, never."

They trudged back to Bradmore Road, silent with mortification. Harriet clenched her fists in an agony of embarrassment and screwed up her face as she thought how foolish she had made herself appear. At Bradmore Road Polly opened the door to them. "Your aunt's to tea today, Miss Harriet," she announced, with a sidelong look at the drawing room door. "Your ma said as to be sure you combed your hair nicely like."

"In that case, there is no need for me to stay," said Miss Edale with something like relief, and she hurried off, as though by leaving Harriet behind she could forget how painful the afternoon had been.

The atmosphere in the drawing room seemed rather strained, as it tended to be when Mrs. Jessop and her sister-in-law were together. Aunt Louisa, gray, bony, severe, sat very stiffly on the edge of her chair; Mrs. Jessop fiddled rather irritably with the tea kettle on its little spirit lamp. Even Dr. Jessop seemed in low spirits, but this was probably because he was obliged today to drink his tea from the little china cup that he so detested. Everybody seemed relieved when Harriet came in.

"Well, Hetty," said her father. "Been touring that museum again today? Beats me what you and Miss Edale find to look at in it. Still, it keeps you out of mischief I suppose. What did you see in it today? Any professors' children, eh?"

Crimson with embarrassment at the memory of the professor's children she had seen, Harriet went over to her aunt and received a chill kiss on her forehead. But Aunt Louisa's mind was obviously on something else. She motioned Harriet out of the way and leaned forward toward her brother.

"It is a scandal to the British people," she said in ringing tones. "A blot on our good name forevermore. We abolish slavery—and do this."

Dr. Jessop emptied his cup at one gulp, and lying back in his armchair, pushed it over toward his wife as a sign that it wanted refilling. "Oh, look here, Lou, steady on, steady on. Why should it be slavery in America and not slavery here for the wretched elephant?"

"A circus," said Aunt Louisa with high drama. "An innocent animal is in our protection, safe and secure at the London Zoological Gardens, and we sell it, like a piece of meat, to a circus. What greater slavery could there be than that! What greater defilement! An American circus too."

"Oh, I don't know," said her brother. "Don't know that I wouldn't mind a bit of it myself. Warmth and security. They say the Yankees are better about warmth than we are in old England."

"William," said Aunt Louisa very witheringly, "how can you bring yourself to talk so flippantly? A long sea voyage, and then a circus at the other end, Barnum's Circus. Apart from anything else, we have our duty to a defenseless animal."

"Why did we bring it over from Africa, then?" demanded Dr. Jessop. "Alice, surely the tea isn't as weak as this already. How many spoonsful did you put in?"

"Papa," said Harriet, who had been sitting there listening, trying to follow the argument. "You're not talking about Jumbo, are you? It isn't Jumbo that's going to America?"

She remembered seeing Jumbo at the Zoological Gardens during the one visit she had made to London with her mother. She had fed him with buns.

Aunt Louisa pointed a dramatic finger at her. "There, William, there speaks the voice of the English child for you. We adults are too cynical and hardened to see the truth of the matter; we must listen to the children!"

Harriet had completely forgotten her unfortunate encounter with the Smiths in her dismay. "Papa, it isn't Jumbo?" she persisted, remembering all at once the newspaper placards, and what her father had read out from the *Oxford Mail*.

"It is." Dr. Jessop eyed the watery fluid in his cup with deep dismay. "But don't you bother your little head abut it. There are other elephants in the world, and in the Zoological Gardens, for that matter."

"William, how can you be so utterly lacking in all feelings of humanity?" Aunt Louisa was leaning forward now, grasping the arms of her chair.

"Now, now, Lou," said Dr. Jessop with good humor. "There are plenty of people who cross the Atlantic. You don't work yourself up about them. Why do it about an elephant? Much better be an elephant, I'd say. No ticket to buy, no encumbrances to bother about, escorted to the ship at one end, met at the other. Can't see what the fuss is about myself." He buried his face in his cup and looked at her over the top of it. "And I'm as fond of animals as any man," he added, prodding the drowsy Dalmatian with his foot. "Wouldn't you say so, Fairy, my girl?"

"But Papa, what are they going to do to Jumbo?" asked Harriet.

Her mother put in a word for the first time. "Now, Harriet, if you had only read the newspapers as I have wished you to do, you would know all about this. Not that I consider it a particularly important item of news, as I have said to your aunt, but it certainly has been fully reported in the *Morning Post* the last few days."

"What has happened, Hetty," said Dr. Jessop, putting down his teacup, "is that the London Zoological Gardens have found that Jumbo is getting out of control and they have sold him to Mr. Barnum of New York for his circus."

"Oh, but Papa," said Hetty, leaving her rock bun untasted in her agitation. "Jumbo! He's so friendly. He ate all the six buns I bought for him, and then the paper bag afterward. How *could* they want to send him to America?"

Miss Jessop looked at her brother triumphantly. "It is with the help of children like this that I shall save that wretched animal from his fate. I shall set on foot a children's crusade. Surely the sight of tens of thousands of weeping children will melt the heart of the Zoological Society." Then she turned to Harriet with such violence that her plate fell from her lap to the ground. "And you, Harriet, shall lead it!"

Chapter 3

The Dog and the Smiths

Harriet thought of nothing for the rest of the week but the Smiths and the elephant. For the first time in her life she began to read the pages of the newspaper that her mother selected and put out for her. (Her mother wished her to be well informed; her father, though he said it was a queer idea to encourage young girls to read newspapers, gave in as long as he had read every inch of it before it was handed over.) Not that she paid the least attention to the main news items—what she was searching for was Jumbo. There were angry and outraged letters in the correspondence column every day, and she drank them in, feeling more angry and outraged herself with every word she read, and furious that she was so helpless to do anything about it.

She was even more helpless as far as the Smiths were concerned, for Miss Edale was laid up with a severe attack of bronchitis, brought on, she thought, by standing about in Canterbury Lane in the piercing February cold, and there were no more walks after school; instead, Polly met her, and hurried her home. Half of her wanted to see the Smiths again, and the other half thought that she could never bear to—it would be too embarrassing. But she found it rather boring with so much extra time on her hands. She finished *Miss Patty* and gave it back to Agatha, and, trying to absorb a few facts, as her mother had suggested, began on *A Child's History of England*. It was a weary business though, and she was quite glad when her mother, on Saturday morning, called her to help with the addressing of envelopes appealing for money for The League of Women's Rights. There were a great many to get through, and it was fun to study the various names and addresses and try to visualize the sort of household that lay behind them. Besides, Saturday was such a long, dull day, without anything to do. But after half an hour or so her hand began aching, and felt icy from perpetually slithering over the cold surface of the envelope and the table, and her attention began to wander.

" 'Miss Louisa Jessop'?" she read out, sitting back in her chair, and stretching her hand to try to ease it a little. "But is Aunt Louisa interested in women, Mama? I thought she liked only animals."

"We must not stop our efforts to put serious things in Louisa's way," said her mother tartly. "Besides," she added after a pause, "she sends me circulars appealing for the Cab Horses' Holiday Fund."

Harriet wondered for a moment what her aunt would do with the circular. She'll probably use the blank side of the paper for writing a notice about her Cab Horses, she thought. Or about the elephant. Then she looked at the long list of names and addresses that she had yet to write, sighed, and finished two more envelopes. She put down her pen again.

"Mama," she said, "I can't read this. There are some people called Anstey. But is it Milk and Ham Street they live in? It sounds very queer."

"Harriet, you are too old to try to be funny," said her mother in an abstracted way.

"But Mama," said Harriet, hurt. "I wasn't. It *looks* like Milk and Ham, but I know it can't be."

"Very well. Bring it here, then." Mrs. Jessop pushed her spectacles firmly on her nose, and scrutinized her handwriting with a frown. "You had better look in the League's address book. You will find it in the middle drawer of my desk."

Elated that her mother had treated her seriously, Harriet took her time. Everything was beautifully ordered in her mother's desk. The pencils lay in a long line, graded in size; there was the sealing apparatus with delicious-looking sticks of wax and tapers, red morocco boxes labeled in gold letters "rubber bands," "paper clips," "pen nibs," and sheets of crisp, untouched paper. The paper was tantalizing; Harriet longed to settle down and write a book.

The address book was bound in black leather. Harriet opened it and began looking through it for Mrs. Anstey's address. A written sheet of paper fell out and slowly floated to the ground. Harriet bent to pick it up, and noticed that it was a letter in her mother's handwriting with the Bradmore Road address on top.

"Mama, here's a letter you have forgotten to post," she began. Then her eyes traveled down it. She was always being scolded for her curiosity, but this time she really could not help it. It was a letter expressing Mrs. Jessop's deep sympathy upon the death of somebody's husband.

"But Mama," she burst out. "Dr. Henry is not dead, is he? I saw him on the way home from school yesterday. But you've written to Mrs. Henry saying you are so sorry that he is."

"By the age of eleven, Harriet, you should surely have learned that to read other people's correspondence is extraordinarily ill-bred," said her mother calmly without raising her head.

"I'm very sorry, Mama. Shall I put this letter in an envelope and address it, then? But Dr. Henry must have died very suddenly."

"He is not dead, so far as I know, and I must have forgotten to put that letter away with the others."

Just as Harriet had opened her mouth to ask more questions about it and then shut it again because she was afraid of being told how curious she was, there came a clatter of boots down the hall, and Dr. Jessop flung open the door and made a loud shivering noise.

"How you women manage to push a pen in this room beats me. It feels like a mortuary."

"One only has to work hard enough, William, and one forgets such things as cold. Besides, we are not invalids, and as you know, it is against my principles to light the drawing room fire before three o'clock."

"Well, I'm glad I haven't got principles like yours, I must say. And why is my little Hetty looking so astonished and as if she is burning to ask a million questions?" Dr. Jessop strode across the room and looked down over Harriet's shoulder at the letter she was holding. "Why, old Henry's not dead. I saw him this morning. Why ever have you written this, Alice?"

Mrs. Jessop, without a sign of being put out, raised her head. "Dr. Henry is elderly. He may well not live very much longer. It is as well to be prepared for such things. I have a number of similar letters in my desk."

Dr. Jessop put his head back and guffawed with laughter. "Well, well, Alice, you're a wonderful woman and no mistake. I always knew how keen you were on doing things ahead, but it never struck me that you would say how sorry you were people had died before the breath was out of them." He slapped his thigh and laughed more than ever. "What principle do you work on?" he asked when he had recovered some of his breath. "Write a letter every time somebody has a seventieth birthday, or do you do it when you see them looking rather shaky?"

Mrs. Jessop tranquilly resumed her correspondence. "It is a scheme which many people who are as busy as I am would find well worth their while to adopt."

"Well, I hope not many of our friends do it—that's all I can say. I shouldn't like to think of my obituary lying about in people's desks. Why, our little Hetty might have easily popped this into an envelope and sent it off, and then where'd you be?" At the thought of this, Dr. Jessop gave another guffaw of laughter and wiped his eyes with a red silk handkerchief.

"In that case Harriet would have had to have asked Mrs. Henry to return the envelope unopened. Well, Harriet, have you found Mrs. Anstey's address?"

"It's Melksham Street," said Harriet, rather disappointed at this tame explanation of Milk and Ham.

"Come now, don't you think Hetty has done enough work for a morning, and a cold morning at that?" Dr. Jessop carefully returned his handkerchief to his breast pocket, arranging it so that a red silk ear showed. "I came along to ask if you could spare her for a ride in the gig with me while I pay one or two calls. She'll be company for me, and she has a dull enough time of it, poor lass."

Harriet looked pleadingly at her mother, her pen poised over the envelope for Mrs. Anstey, slowly dripping ink on it. "Yes, Harriet may go," said Mrs. Jessop. "I am afraid she really has not the application to persevere with this task."

"Have a heart, Alice," said Dr. Jessop jovially. "She's only a child, and is it your Women's Rights you've given her to do? If it was an appeal to buy buns for Jumbo now, then you'd see how she could work. Eh, Hetty? Run along now, there's a good girl, and get your hat, I told them to have the gig ready by eleven o'clock, and it's five to the hour now."

Harriet, warmly dressed, and with her hands inside the muff that her father had given her for Christmas, skipped along the road by his side in the direction of the livery stables where the gig and the black mare, Jess, were kept. Fairy, with an alert nose and tail, trotted briskly at their heels. The gig was ready waiting for them, the brass lanterns gleaming, the coachwork of the sides polished to mirror-brightness. Jess, immaculately groomed, fidgeted impatiently between the shafts. Dr. Jessop greeted Jess, checked over the details of the harness, adjusted the curb chain, and made approving sounds. "Well, I must say you do things better here than they did back in the north," he said to the Irish groom who held the mare's head. It was the same groom that always accompanied Dr. Jessop on his rounds, though more often than not the doctor preferred to drive himself. He was exceedingly proud of his turnout, and stead-fastly refused to change it for a brougham. So the brougham which Great-Uncle Harry had used was laid up in the stables while Dr. Jessop did his rounds in the gig. He paid close attention to every detail, down to the elegant horse rug that Jess wore with his initials on it, and the checked rug that he put over his knees to drive. He had even specially selected Fairy for her suitability as a carriage dog.

He handed Harriet up into the gig, and tucked the rug around her knees. "You're going to find it a bit cold, my lass. But I suppose it's not so cold as that drawing room. Your mother's a wonderful woman, but her heating apparatus is quite different from ours."

He swung himself up beside Harriet, and settled himself, pulling on his driving gloves. "Yes, your mother's a wonderful woman," he said again as the gig turned out into the Banbury road. "There can't be many like her. I've never known her to be late on one single occasion, and you know what most women are like for keeping you waiting—take your Aunt Lou-isa, for instance. Most things your mother does so that they're ready waiting for you long before you think of asking. She always packs the luggage for the holidays a week in advance, and I've even known her buy Christmas presents two years in advance. It's not that she hasn't got enough to do; no woman works harder. Though I think writing poor old Henry's funeral letter is going a bit far, myself." Dr. Jessop began laughing again at the thought of it.

"I know Mama is wonderful," said Harriet in a sad voice; then, in an unusual burst of confidence, for she was always afraid of saying anything serious to her father in case he laughed at her, she added: "I do wish I could be like her. But I don't think, however old I grow, I could be interested in the same things. I mean causes, and that sort of thing. I do wish that I had a cause that I could get really interested in—it must be so exciting."

"Now, now, Hetty, don't you go bothering your head about causes," said her father. "And don't you go looking out for them. Some day one'll just fall down in front of you—like that." He snapped his fingers. "And then's the time to start getting excited about it. Anyway, you're far too young to go fussing about them yet. Now look, I've an idea. You stop worrying about whether you're going to turn out like your mother, and I'll buy you a new dress. I've seen just the thing for you in one of those big shops in the High Street—pale blue with frills behind. I tell you what—next Tuesday, I won't be free till them, I'll come and collect you from school myself and we'll go and buy it. Now, what do you say to that?"

"Oh, Papa," said Harriet, taking both hands out of her muff to clutch his arm.

"Well then, not a word to your mother, eh? We'll dress you up in it and give her a surprise."

Harriet sat in a stupor of happiness the whole length of the Banbury road. To have a pale blue dress and Papa calling for her! She had always secretly hoped that one day he would pass by in the gig when they were all coming out of school so that she could say to Agatha and the others, "There's Papa."

With brisk, high steps the mare trotted down the Banbury

road, the way that Harriet and Miss Edale always trudged on
their afternoon walks. But the road looked quite different from
a seat in the gig; you could see better into the front gardens, for
one thing. They drove past St. Giles Church, where the Banbury
road met the road to Woodstock and the joined fork made the
broad street called St. Giles. It looked as though Dr. Jessop
were heading for the old part of the town, the University part,
but Harriet dared not ask him—she was too afraid of being
disappointed. Occasionally she glanced back to see if Fairy was
following. Her father never bothered to do this; he was too
certain of her—his horses and his dogs were always beautifully
trained. The gig turned smartly to the right. "Balliol College,"
said her father, nodding to a building on the corner. "That's
one of the most famous colleges in Oxford. You'd better mark it
down."

Harriet stared at it with greedy eyes; it was only the second
college whose name she knew. Then the gig turned left, and
she felt a surge of excitement—they were getting near Canterbury Lane. The Smiths might be anywhere about. She could
not decide whether it was pleasure or horror that she was
feeling at the thought of it, but she sat tense in her seat and
gripped the side of the gig until her hand hurt. The streets were
full of young men in black gowns hurrying and jostling. They
paid no attention whatever to traffic on the road, and slipped
under the mare's nose as if she were invisible. Muttering to
himself, Dr. Jessop picked his way through them, turned again,
and there they were in Canterbury Lane itself.

"Is it going to be a long call, Papa?" she asked in a frightened
voice, wondering what the Smiths would say this time if they
passed and saw her in their road again.

"Shouldn't be too long, m'dear, if the lady isn't talkative.
I've never set eyes on her before, so I can't tell."

Then it came over Harriet, with a sick feeling, that there
were only two houses in the street where a lady could be living,

the Smiths' and the house next to it. And whichever it was, the Smith boys would be able to see her sitting there outside.

"I'll get them to ask you in, Hetty. It's too cold for you to be sitting out here—and Alice says there are three boys. And, by the by, weren't you asking me the other day whether I knew any professors with children? I didn't then, but I do now."

"Oh no, Papa," said Harriet in a trembling voice. "I'd rather stay here, thank you very much."

"Afraid they'd be too rough for you, those boys, eh? Well, maybe you're right. But you'll get very cold, poor lass. Mind you keep that rug tucked well around you. I'll try to be as quick as I can. Tell you what—if the room they show me into faces down over the street, I'll give you a signal through the window. Watch out for it, mind."

Chuckling loudly, Dr. Jessop tossed over the reins to the groom, reached behind him for his bag, and jumped down into the street. He gave a loud knock with the brass knocker on the door of the house where Harriet knew the Smiths lived, and turned around to wink comically at Harriet.

"Oh, Pat," he called to the Irish groom. "Watch out that this dog doesn't get around Jess's heels." He indicated a very hairy, muddy-looking animal that was waiting near the door, wagging its tail cheerfully at him. "She doesn't care for dogs, except Fairy, and even old Fairy takes care to keep out of her reach."

Then a smart parlormaid with streamers on her cap opened the door, and Dr. Jessop disappeared into the house. The dog, with an air of relief after a long wait, trotted in after him. Harriet sat bold upright in the gig, feeling horribly exposed. She buried her chin in her collar, and stared fixedly at the floorboards.

It seemed an age that she sat like that, and she began to grow stiff and numb. Then she remembered what her father had said about a signal. Perhaps she had better look up, just in case. She scanned the windows of the house, starting at the bottom. But they were all veiled in white lace, and it would be quite impossible to see if anybody was behind them. Then she reached the third flight of windows. There was one there that lacked its lace curtain, and as she peered at it, a red head was poked out, and a voice said loudly, "It *is* that girl again. I told you it was."

Before she had time to collect her wits, a second head poked out.

"So it is," said another voice. "One up to you, James."

"Why is she always here spying on us?" said the first voice peevishly.

"I don't know. Let's go down and ask her. Madam, your presence irks us, I shall say."

"Thomas, she'll hear you. Come in," Harriet faintly heard a third, muffled voice say from within the room. But by that time she was staring in a fever at the floor of the gig, her fists clenched inside her muff, as she willed with all the concentration that she possessed, that her father should stop whatever he was doing inside, and come out instantly.

"Well, I'm going down anyway," she heard the first voice say, but more faintly this time. "Stop pulling me, Joshua. All right, I won't say anything, but I want to see if that spotted dog is real or a stuffed one. Let *go*."

The window slammed. She heard no more, and sat there in a tremble of fright, waiting for the street door to burst open and a horde of boys to pour out. A minute or so later it did open, but not with so much violence as she had expected. Then, with an enormous surge of relief, she heard her father's voice.

"Well, well, my boyo, you're in a hurry this fine morning. What's it all about, eh? Are you coming out to see my good spotted dog? Love me, love my dog, I always say. Ah, she's a good lass. Look at her sitting there so patiently."

Bolder now in her relief, Harriet looked up. There was her father smiling down benevolently at the red-headed James Smith. And there was the other dog, looking as muddy and as disheveled as ever, wagging his tail and grinning by their feet. "Here," said her father, "you'd better keep this animal of yours inside now. It's getting in a fine state in this dirty street. A fine mess it's made of your mother's room too. You ought to school it better, young man."

Harriet trembled at the way her father was treating the formidable James Smith. What would he say to that? But a new voice broke in, and peering into the dimness of the hall beyond the street door, she saw the red face of Professor Smith. He sounded almost savage.

"*Our* dog, did you say? I wouldn't have the hair of one within the door, if I could help it. Do you mean to say that this animal is not yours?"

Dr. Jessop became indignant in his turn. "What, this ill-bred cur? There's my dog, sitting under the gig like a statue, and I'll wage you all Lombardy Street to a China orange that she hasn't budged from there since I left her." He had Professor Smith by the arm now, and was pointing to Fairy. "Has she, Hetty? You'll vouch for her. Well, speak up, my lass."

"No, Papa," said Hetty in a quavering voice. "I don't think she's moved." Behind the burly figure of Professor Smith she could now see the tall Thomas, with Joshua peering around his shoulder.

"Well, as far as looks go," said Professor Smith, who seemed to be recovering his good humor, "I can't say I see much between the two. I never have cared for spots, and I confess these make me dizzy. Besides, the animal's got a pink nose—extremely degenerate, I should say."

This touched Dr. Jessop on his most sensitive spot. He was a man of the utmost good humor, except where his animals were concerned. "Degenerate, did you say? Let me tell you that this Dalmatian is out of Brandon Betsy of Wildboarclough by Wincle Winner. And Winner was sired by Fallowfield Ferox himself."

"My dear fellow," said Professor Smith, "I don't care whether he is sired by Jumbo of the London Zoological Gardens. I merely remarked that I did not care for his appearance. No genealogical tables can change my opinion on that point."

"The animal," said Dr. Jessop, slamming his hat down on his head, "is a bitch." He brushed aside James, who was doubled up with laughter and muttering, "Jumbo of the London Zoological Gardens," and strode to the gig, where the groom, looking rather alarmed, handed him over the reins, and scrambled to his own place. With his jaw set fiercely, Dr. Jessop backed Jess, turned the trap, and drove off up Canterbury Lane without another glance toward the Smiths.

Nothing was said. He picked his way through the traffic and the undergraduates ruthlessly, not caring how many close shaves he gave the indolent young men who behaved as though the roads belonged to them alone. It was not until they reached the Banbury road that he relaxed the ferocious expression on his face. "D'you know, Hetty, it really would be rather funny, if only that stiff-necked fool of a professor hadn't been so insulting about Fairy." He slapped his hand on his leg and let out a shout of laughter. "Oh, it really was very funny, you know, very funny." He became so convulsed with laughter that he stopped the gig and sat there, quivering and shaking until Harriet looked at him with alarm. "That dog," he said, "followed me into the house as bold as brass. Up the stairs we went into my lady's bedroom. He stood there and shook himself— water flying all over the place. Well, thought I, better not say anything, she's probably one of the sort that's very touchy about her precious Bonzo. Then bless me if the beast didn't jump up on to the bed—beautiful snowy-white bedspread, y'know—and *rolled* on it, all over it, in fact. Well, I wasn't going to have that. I'm all in favor of a bit of dirt, but I thought that was carrying things a bit far. Enough's enough, I said to myself. So I pushed him off and asked my lady's pardon. I mean, people don't like having their dogs told off—don't like it myself. And all the time I was talking to the good lady, there he was running around the room tearing at things with his teeth and putting his feet up on to all the chairs. I should think every piece of furniture in that room has got the brute's paw marks on it now. Well, well, well, that professor fellow can be as superior as he likes about Fairy, but the laugh's on him when he sees the state of that room." He gave one final guffaw of laughter, and then picked up the reins and drove on. "But that poor lady," he said. "All the time too polite to say, 'take your horrible dog out of my room.' " He sighed. "What it is to be too polite! Still, at any rate, it's something that can't be said for her husband."

Or for her sons, thought Harriet dolefully.

Chapter 4

Harriet Attacks

*T*he upshot of all this was not to make Harriet think any the worse of the Smith boys, or of Professor Smith, though she was thoroughly alarmed by them all, but to make her wish miserably that her father had not behaved as he did, and then to feel even more miserable at wishing it. But if only, she thought, he had not talked so excitedly about Fairy, when it was perfectly clear that all the Smiths despised dogs. The worst of it was that it had spoiled her excitement about the new dress that was to be bought. She even half hoped that her father would forget about it because she felt so ashamed of taking it from him in her present mood.

But on Tuesday morning her father looked up from the paper, spread untidily over the breakfast table in front of him. "What about our little errand this afternoon, Hetty?" he said.

"Are we still going, Papa?" she asked rather nervously.

"Of course we are. And why not? Three o'clock sharp and I'll be outside your school."

Harriet hesitated, and then she burst out. "Papa, need Fairy come too?" It had come over her during the last few days how very odd it must look, the huge black and white dog trotting after the gig wherever it went.

Dr. Jessop was amazed. "Fairy not come too? Of course she will, won't you, my good spotted dog? She gets in nobody's way, and whatever would she do at home all by herself?"

"No, you must take the dog with you, William," said Mrs. Jessop firmly. "She howls without stopping if you're away from the house for long. Are you going to be in for tea?"

"Harriet and I will be back to tea. But we have a little business to transact first. And of course I'm taking Fairy with me, why ever not? Love me, love my dog, you know, Harriet."

And Harriet, who bitterly regretted now that she had ever said anything about the dog, blushed and was silent.

She could see the gig parked exactly opposite the school gate as she came out of the door, and could just make out through the spokes of the wheel the figure of Fairy, who sat there like stone. She lingered on the path, hoping that some of the girls from her class would catch her up with and see the gig, but her father caught sight of her before any of them had appeared.

"Hello there, Hetty," he called. "Come along." And then, as she hurried up, he said, "I promised your mother we wouldn't be long. She seems to think your Aunt Louisa is coming, and she's not too keen on entertaining her by herself. I expect we'll find them tearing each other to pieces when we get in. Besides, I want my tea. I can tell you, you're a lucky girl; nothing has ever come between me and my tea before."

"Not even a patient, Papa?"

"Not even a patient. Oh well, let me see, there was a man who was mad and violent on the doorstep of our old house, and I had to leave off my tea at the fifth cup to stop him breaking the place up and giving them hysterics in the kitchen."

They drove into the crowded middle of Oxford, and Dr. Jessop halted the gig outside a big draper's with a great many windows. "There," he said, nodding toward one of the windows. "There's the dress. Like it?"

The only child's dress in that window was a pale blue one, trimmed with rows of white braid, and fastened with a long line of tiny pearl buttons. "Oh, Papa," Harriet said with awe in her voice. "Do you mean that one?"

"That was what I thought, but I want to know what you think."

"Oh, it's lovely. But it's so different from anything else that I wear," she faltered.

"All the better for that. Your clothes are a bit sober for my taste. Your mother's a very sensible woman, and I'm sure she does it from the best motives, but I'd like to see a bit of color now and again."

"But do you think Mama will mind?"

"You tell her that you'll make it into frocks for her Prisoners' babies when you've finished with it, and in the meantime you can put it on when you're with me."

Dr. Jessop strode into the shop and leaned confidentially over the first counter that he saw. "I want that blue dress in the window for my little girl here."

Harriet was fascinated, it was so different from the sort of shopping she did with her mother, who would finger material, compare prices, and cross-examine the shop assistants about quality at half a dozen shops before she finally bought something.

There was a great deal of bustling, and a tall, thin, drooping young man had eventually to be called upon to thread his way through the dresses in the shop window and very delicately reach over a purple one embroidered with black bugles to pick out the blue dress right in front. Harriet eyed her father nervously while all this was going on, half afraid that he would become so impatient for his tea that he would stride out.

"Here is the dress, sir," said a lady assistant at last. "But is it the right size for your little girl?"

"Oh, I expect it will do. Looks all right to me," said Dr. Jessop, feeling in all his pockets for his wallet.

"But don't you think the young lady had better try it on? It is a small fitting, and it might not be big enough." The saleslady was stout, with a back of terrifying stiffness. She had a high color and cheeks that puffed out as though she were perpetually blowing. Harriet found her very awe-inspiring, and, fearful of a scene, she tugged at her father's arm.

"Oh, please, Papa," she said. "Do let me try it on."

With the saleslady sweeping majestically ahead of her, she was led to a stuffy little room with mirrors on every wall. Facing the window, so that she could not catch a glimpse of herself in a glass before she was dressed to the last button, she tore off her gray wool dress with desperate haste, and pulled on the little blue dress. It was a hard struggle to get into it, but at last, panting and gasping, she got her head clear.

"It isn't too small, is it?" she said urgently to the saleslady, who stood by, frowning and pursing her lips at such frantic haste.

"If you will do up the buttons, Miss, then perhaps we can see."

Harriet fumbled with the scores of little buttons that fastened the bodice, and then looked at herself at last in the mirrors. She could hardly recognize herself. She looked the sort of child that she had always wanted to be. The stout lady came over and examined the fit of the dress with pursed lips. Harriet watched her anxiously, hoping she would not notice that the dress was a little tight under the arms.

"Well, I hope you're not the growing sort, Miss," she said at last. "It doesn't leave you much room."

"Oh, but it's quite long," Harriet assured her, "and I don't grow very fast, really. I've had that gray dress for two years now."

"Hmm," said the stout lady. "Well, we'd better see what your pa says."

Dr. Jessop was striding up and down the shop impatiently when Harriet pattered down the stairs and presented herself to him. "Papa, do you like it?" she said self-consciously. The shop lady followed her with slow, dignified steps, the gray dress, now suddenly looking very drab and shabby, folded neatly over her arm.

"It does not allow the little girl a great deal of room," she began.

"Never mind, never mind," said Dr. Jessop impatiently. "It looks all right to me. Where's your coat, Hetty?"

"Can I go home in it, then?" Harriet went red with pleasure.

"Waste of time taking it off. Besides, I bought it for you to wear, didn't I?"

So a parcel was made of the gray dress, its shabbiness contrasting rather pathetically with the new crisp sheet of brown paper, and the whiteness of the string. Rather reluctantly, Harriet put on her coat.

"You do like it, don't you, Papa?" she said as she hurried out of the shop with him.

"Never seen you look so nice. Come along, tea, tea. I've never been so thirsty in my life. Must be all the shopping. If I were your mother I'd buy a hundredweight of potatoes and a hundredweight of tea, and tell the butcher to send mutton chops every day, and never do any shopping from one week to the next."

"Oh, Papa. Shouldn't I have tried the dress then?"

"I had to let you do that, I suppose, if only to stop that stout party having a fit of apoplexy. That would have kept me from my tea even longer—we'd have had to have found someone else to pay the money to. Come on, Jess, my girl, you show us how quickly you can get home."

The afternoon was gray and cold, and inside the shops the

lights were on, though there was still some time to go before dusk fell. The mare trotted smartly up Cornmarket Street. Dr. Jessop kept his eyes rigidly in front of him in case, as he said, he should see a patient and fail to recognize him. "I can't stand nonsense about hurt feelings and suchlike," he said. Harriet, however, let her eyes rove around, examining the dresses of other girls of her own age, and thinking how very much nicer her new dress was than any of the coats they were wearing. In a warm burst of gratefulness she slipped her hand out of her muff and hugged her father's arm.

It was then that she heard, above all the street sounds, a sort of chanting. She looked at the pavement on her left, and there—the gig was just passing them—stood the three Smith boys, and now she heard more clearly what they were shouting.

"Brandon Betsy of Wildboarclough!"

"Fallowfield Ferox himself!"

"Jumbo of the London Zoological Gardens!"

They were so close that Harriet could have pulled their noses. She saw the tall boy bowing elaborately, the middle one giggling, and James leaping up and down and bawling breathlessly about Jumbo of the London Zoological Gardens. Her father gave them a quick sideways look. Harriet was trembling with fury. She would have leaned out and boxed their ears, but it was too late now. Casting her eyes around wildly, grinding her teeth that the whip was out of her reach, she caught sight of the parcel they had made of her old dress. It was lying on the seat beside her. She snatched it up, knelt on the seat, and hurled the parcel with as much force as she could gather, into the knot of boys, now some yards behind.

Dr. Jessop hauled the mare to a halt. "Gracious heavens, Hetty, whatever has happened?" he demanded.

"Drive on, Papa," she said wildly. Then, stamping her foot on the floor of the gig, she repeated, "Oh, please, please, drive on."

Dr. Jessop was a man who thought words, and in particular arguments, were rather useless, so he drove on, and Harriet sat tense beside him, not daring to look behind her. She had an idea that the parcel had bounced off James's stomach, but she was not sure. Anyway, she wished that the parcel had been harder, that it had held half a dozen flatirons.

"My word, Hetty," said Dr. Jessop as they approached the St. Giles churchyard standing in the middle of the fork made by the Banbury and the Woodstock roads, "you are in a fury. What was it all about?"

"Boys," said Harriet between clenched teeth. "Horrible boys. How could they be so horrible!"

"So horrible as what? Who were they, anyway?" But Harriet was silent. "Was it the Smith boys?" her father pursued. "I thought I saw them in Cornmarket Street." He turned to look at Harriet. "They're all right. What were they doing, pulling faces at you?" He looked at her furious face with amusement, and then glanced down at the seat beside her, which seemed curiously empty. "What have you done with that parcel? We had it there when we started—I'm positive of that."

"I threw it at them," she said defiantly.

Dr. Jessop threw back his head and bellowed with laughter. Then he slapped his knee with his gloved hand and laughed louder still. "You threw it at them! Well Hetty, that's rich—that really is. Was it because you hated the boys or you hated the dress?"

"It was because of the boys," she said in a stifled voice.

"And did you hit them?"

"I think it hit the little boy, the one with red hair. I'm glad it was him; he was laughing the loudest."

"Hetty," said Dr. Jessop. "You take care. That's how your Aunt Louisa feels about people who try to do down her cab horses. She'd like to put them on the rack if she could, or roll them downhill in a barrel full of nails. Only of course she doesn't do it—but you do. It's lucky for the world at large that you haven't got a cause yet to get worked up about, as you were lamenting the other day." Then he threw back his head and shouted with laughter again. "Well, well, we are a pair. I let muddy dogs loose all over Mrs. Smith; you throw parcels at her boys. I can tell you one thing—we'll never be allowed to cross the threshold of *that* door again."

In all this passion Harriet had quite forgotten about her new dress. It was only when she had got home and was standing taking off her coat in the passage where the coat pegs were that she remembered. Her arms felt more unprotected than usual from the cold that seemed to strike up from the black and white tiles on the floor. She looked down at them, and there was her pale blue dress, looking a little out of place now in the Jessop house, where everything was so sensible and so plain. In spite of the cold she lingered. Perhaps in a minute or so her aunt would have gone—she had glimpsed her standing in the drawing room in her outdoor clothes looking as though she were on the point of departure. She felt suddenly very self-conscious about the new dress and did not want to face more people in it than she need. Dr. Jessop came clumping down the stairs.

"Come on, come on, Hetty, wake up out of your dream, or you'll die of cold standing there."

Harriet followed him, smoothing down her dress, and suddenly conscious of a draft under her arm. She was dreadfully afraid she must have burst that seam as she threw the parcel. Aunt Louisa and Mrs. Jessop wheeled around as Harriet and her father came into the drawing room.

"Well, Alice, what do you think of our afternoon's work?" said Dr. Jessop, looking at Harriet with great satisfaction. "Stand up, lass, and show yourself. This wasn't how you behaved in the shop."

Harriet unfolded her arms, with which she was covering as

much of the dress as she could. "There's quite a lot of length to it, Mama," she said anxiously, looking at her mother.

"Come along, Alice, what d'you think of it?" demanded Dr. Jessop impatiently.

"I am just considering. But when in the world is Harriet to wear it?"

"When we have company. Sundays. Any time you like."

"She will have to wear a holland pinafore over it then, or it won't keep clean for an instant. I think you ought to go and put one on now, Harriet."

"What do you think of it, Louisa, eh?" Dr. Jessop turned to his sister, hoping that perhaps admiration would come from that quarter.

"A little frivolous perhaps," said Aunt Louisa coolly. "But then I am hardly a judge of these matters."

"Never mind, Hetty—you and I like it, anyway. You just put it on when we're together. Ah, but Alice, your daughter's got spirit, I can tell you. Louisa ought to be pleased about this. Shall I tell them, Hetty?" Harriet, crimson, with tears very near the surface, looked at him blankly. "That gray dress," he went on. "You'll never guess what's become of it."

"Have you made her give it away to one of your poor patients?"

"I haven't made her do anything. But she's given it away all right. Thrown it away, in fact." Dr. Jessop laughed uproariously.

"Pray William, do explain yourself," said Mrs. Jessop with a shade of impatience.

"She threw it out of the gig at three boys," he said trium-phantly. "Now what do you think of that?"

"Is this true, Harriet?"

Harriet nodded miserably.

"Do you know the boys? Though I hardly suppose you do."

"It was Professor Smith's three lads," put in Dr. Jessop.

"Then, Harriet, you will have to call on them and ask them

to return the dress. Now run and get your pinafore. You don't want to get this dress in a mess before you recover the gray one."

But Aunt Louisa was looking at her with more interest and approval than she had ever shown before. "The child has indeed inherited the Jessop spirit," she said. "If she uses it in the proper direction she ought to go far. Use it for the well-being of our suffering brethren, the animals, Harriet," she said dramatically. "Jumbo needs you, and Oxford is a dark and unenlightened place."

"Louisa, I hardly think . . ." said Mrs. Jessop, looking disapproving.

But Aunt Louisa cut her short. "Harriet, you must make it your mission to turn the hearts of Oxford. Our need is urgent. Good-bye William, good-bye Alice. No, I am afraid I cannot stay to tea. I have no time these days for such frivolities when every minute means life for that suffering animal. Harriet, remember, it is to you that I look."

And Harriet went to bed that night with her blue dress forgotten. She had found her cause; as her father said, it had dropped right at her feet. She would work for Jumbo with every ounce of her energy, and she would fight those Smith boys to the death. How she would set about it she did not yet know. But she was sure the ways and means would drop at her feet just as the cause itself had done.

Chapter 5

Aunt Louisa Attacks

Before Harriet could begin to dedicate herself to Jumbo there was the unfortunate affair of the dress to be gotten over. She could never hope that her mother would forget it; Mrs. Jessop had never been known to forget anything, and Harriet, lying in bed that next morning, tormented herself with thoughts of the horror that lay ahead of her. The only glimmer of hope was that her father had to pay another call there, and could do the asking himself.

But Mrs. Jessop had other ideas. She raised her head from her correspondence at breakfast. "Oh, Harriet," she said. "Miss Edale is still ill, it seems, and in any case does not wish to go out for walks until the winter is over. The fuss that people make about the weather is incomprehensible to me; it is a sure sign, to my mind, of not having enough to do. But your Aunt Louisa has suggested that you should accompany her until Miss Edale can take charge, and she will meet you after school. It is not an arrangement that altogether pleases me, but I think it is better than sending Polly to meet you every afternoon when she can ill be spared. I will ask your aunt to take you to Canterbury Lane this afternoon to inquire about the dress. Something must be done about it without delay."

"But Mama, what shall I say?" Harriet faltered.

"Ask to see the three boys, and request them to return you the parcel, it seems."

"Couldn't I ask for Mrs. Smith?"

"Was it Mrs. Smith that you threw it at?"

Harriet, wondering wildly whether it would be worse if it had been Mrs. Smith, had to admit that this was not so.

"Then presumably Mrs. Smith knows nothing about it, and you would be wasting your time to ask her," said Mrs. Jessop crisply. "I am sorry, my dear Harriet, but I know very little of the circumstances in which this happened, and I am afraid I can help you no further."

Harriet's thoughts were far too occupied with the ordeal in front of her to pay very much attention at school that day, and she sat through her lessons in a stupor, quite blind to the fact that the rest of the class had reached a new chapter of the Book of Kings, so that when her turn came to read, she read about Jehu and Jezebel instead of about Jehu writing letters, and was very sharply reprimanded.

Dragging out of school, she remembered Jehu's words, "Who is on my side, who?" and thought that never was anyone so lacking in people on her side as she was. She had ample time to reflect on this as she stood near the gate waiting for her aunt. Miss Jessop was always late. She was never ashamed of this; she said it came from having too full a day and trying to crowd in too many duties. In her opinion, she said, one could waste a tremendous amount of time over the years by being two minutes early for every appointment, whereas no appointment suffered if one was two minutes late for it. (Except the person who was kept waiting, Dr. Jessop had once remarked.) However, on this occasion she was a good deal more than two minutes late, and the last straggling gossip had drifted out of the school door by the time Harriet saw her aunt's gray upright figure advancing on her from the distance.

"Well, Harriet," she said when she got within speaking distance. "Your mother tells me we are to go to Canterbury Lane. Canterbury Lane will do as well as anywhere to begin with."

She did not explain what she meant by this remark, but Harriet, looking at her reticule, which seemed to be bulging with papers, guessed that her aunt must be on one of her animal campaigns. Her aunt had a hand in most of the societies which had anything to do with animals, but chief among them the Domestic Pets' League of Pity, and the Cab Horses' Holiday Fund, and there were always leaflets to distribute and posters to stick up. They walked at a brisk pace through the wet streets of north Oxford, and Harriet heartily wished that the next hour was over, and that they were walking back to the chill comforts of Bradmore Road. Canterbury Lane got disagreeably near; it could not long be staved off now. Then they were on it, and she realized that she had not the slightest idea of what she was going to say, and to whom. Her anger against the boys was raging just as fiercely as it had yesterday, and one of the worst parts of the whole affair was that she would have to eat humble pie when all the time she wanted to hurl herself at them. And she was terribly afraid that she might sob with rage, and that they would think she was just crying.

Aunt Louisa became very busy with the contents of her reticule as they walked down the lane. She was still busy when the Smiths' house was reached.

"This is the house," Harriet said dully.

"Very well, Harriet, just ring the bell while I push one of these through the letter box of the next house. Your friends shall have a leaflet too, but one must not neglect the chance of personal contact as well."

The smart parlormaid with streamers on her cap opened the

door. Before Harriet could open her mouth her aunt took charge of the situation. She was now armed with a notebook in which a long list of names was written, and a purple pencil.

"For or against Jumbo?" she said briskly. "Come, come, girl, which?"

The parlormaid seemed very taken aback. "I beg your pardon, miss?" she said, clinging to the door and seeming quite frightened.

"Jumbo," said Aunt Louisa, "of the London Zoological Gardens. They must feel about it one way or the other in this household. What I want to know is what they feel."

"I'm sure I don't know, to be sure," said the girl nervously. "I'll go and ask the mistress."

"Never mind the mistress just now. What are your own views?" Aunt Louisa smoothed down the page of her notebook and scribbled vigorously. "Well?"

"I don't know, miss," said the maid, biting her lip nervously.

"If you don't know, then you must be 'for.' It is only the depraved and brutal who are against animals."

"Oh, *animals,*" said the maid, as if light had suddenly flooded in where all was dark before. "They don't think much of animals in this house. Except cats. The master allows us to keep a cat in the kitchen because he says mice are worse. There are the chickens too—but then he says he likes eggs, so he puts up with chickens. There aren't any more animals, miss."

"It is not their animals so much as their attitude that matters," said Miss Jessop severely. "However, we will return to that later. Meanwhile, how much are you prepared to contribute?"

"Miss?" faltered the maid.

"I presume they pay you wages, however brutal they are in this household. How much are you going to give out of them to support a poor dumb animal?"

The maid looked really frightened now, and hung on to the

door as though she were afraid Miss Jessop would capture her and hold her to ransom.

"I've only got sixpence till the end of the month," she burst out. "I've sent the rest home to my mother. There's our Sarah Ann, and Lizzy and Johnnie and Alf and Clem still at home, and our mom is fair pushed to feed them and clothe them sometimes," she explained anxiously, frightened perhaps that Miss Jessop would pursue her mother and demand the money back.

Miss Jessop brushed this on one side. "Never mind, girl, sixpence will do. And now I will see your mistress."

The girl fled thankfully. Harriet felt sorry for her. "Aunt Louisa," she said, "I've got a sixpence that Papa gave me last Sunday. You can have that."

"Thank you, Harriet. Every little counts—though of course we must always remember that Jumbo eats ten sixpences every hour that he is awake. Therefore you and this girl between you have kept him alive for only twelve minutes. That is a sobering thought, is it not?"

"But Aunt Louisa," began Harriet, wishing to explain that it was the maid's sixpence that she was trying to save. Then she stopped, thinking that it would seem rather cruel to wish to keep Jumbo alive for only six minutes. At that moment, there was the sound of voices in the passage down which the maid had fled, a man's voice; Professor Smith appeared, looking very disgruntled. "The lady says she wants money," the maid was saying, as she trotted along beside him, looking anxiously toward the front door, as though she were afraid Aunt Louisa might by now have produced a pistol. "For animals, she says."

"It depends what she wants to do to the animals," Professor Smith said wrathfully as he strode up the hall. "If she is floating a company for the abolition of dogs I'll cheerfully buy one thousand shares, and think them cheap at a pound each. Or a society to stop hysterical females filling up the correspondence columns of the daily papers with nonsense about Jumbo."

Miss Jessop had banged her notebook shut, fastened a rubber band around it, and was standing grimly with folded arms, prepared to do battle. Alarmed at what her aunt and the professor might do between them, and wanting to escape at all costs, Harriet brushed past and darted into the hall. "If you please," she said breathlessly to the professor, "could I see Thomas or Joshua or James? They've got a parcel of mine."

Professor Smith barely looked at her. "Take this little girl up to the schoolroom," he said to the maid. Then he strode on to confront Aunt Louisa.

Thankful at being rid of Miss Jessop, the maid scurried up the stairs and turned to Harriet to see if she was following. The first flight and the landing were thickly carpeted, but this turned to oilcloth with the second flight. The maid paused at the bottom and turned around to Harriet again.

"She didn't ought to have come here with her talk about animals, that lady," she said. "I don't mind a bit of them myself, but the master's clean against them, especially dogs, since that one got into the mistress's bedroom when she was ill and made such a mess. Lawks, what a mess it made. It followed the doctor in from the street. I suppose it was his dog."

Before Harriet could correct this outrageous untruth, the maid was scuttling up the stairs again and knocking at a door on the landing above. She put her head around.

"There's a young lady to see you," she announced. Harriet heard the sound of chairs being scraped back and excited muttering. She walked in, holding her head very high.

"You may have picked up a parcel of mine yesterday," she said, trying to sound very calm and distant. The boys were sitting around a tea table, and with them was an elderly woman who might have been their nurse. "Master James," she was saying, "now stop kicking your chair at once, and that's the last time I'm going to tell you."

But by this time James had stopped kicking his chair, and was staring at Harriet with great excitement. "It's the girl with the spotty dog," he announced.

"Fallowfield Ferox," said his eldest brother, pushing back his chair, and staring at Harriet in his turn.

"I have come for my parcel, if you please," said Harriet very haughtily.

"Ho-ho," said Thomas. "Fallowfield Ferocior."

"Oh, Thomas, don't," said Joshua. He had always seemed the mildest of the three boys, but even he was laughing now. "She can't understand."

"Fallowfield the more ferocious. Smith, compare 'ferox.' Ferox Ferocior, but I shouldn't think you could say ferocissimus, so you would have to say maxime ferox. Puella maxime ferox—a most headstrong damsel. Quite right, Smith—full marks."

"Come along, Master Thomas, stop all your fooling around now," interrupted the nurse. "The young lady asked you for something."

"She asked for a parcel, but she threw it at James."

"It hit me in the stomach," announced James.

Nurse was scandalized. "Master James, you know you're not to say that word. And with a lady here too. Now there's to be no jam for your tea today."

"I've had it," said James coolly. "Anyway, it did hit me there, and she threw it, didn't she?"

"I expect it was all a mistake. Young ladies don't throw things."

"She did," said James, scowling.

"Was that the gray dress that I found in the playbox this morning?" said the nurse. "Well now, I wondered what it was doing there. I took it to your mama, I thought it must be something to do with her. Master Joshua, run along now and ask your mama if you can take it from her bedroom. I put it on the big chest of drawers."

Harriet was now left with the two most terrible of the three boys, with only the old nurse to stand between her and them. "Would you like some tea, dear?" she asked Harriet. "Master James will go down and get you a cup and saucer."

For an instant Harriet wondered whether it was worth accepting so that the terrible James could be sent out of the room for a moment or two; then she considered that it would in the end mean spending far longer with him, as she would have to sit down at the table to drink the tea.

"No, thank you," she said hastily.

"How is Bessie Barleymow?" asked Thomas, languidly tilting back his chair.

"Now Master Thomas, you stop tipping that chair, or else we'll have a nasty accident. You're too old for me to be at you all the time," said Nurse severely.

It was unfortunate that Harriet, whose eyes had been roving around the room, should have chosen to look at Thomas at this moment, for he clearly thought she was jeering at him, and his temper became savage.

"I was referring to the spotty, degenerate animal with the pink nose, in case you thought I meant yourself."

Harriet surveyed him with what she hoped was cold dignity. "Fairy is all right, thank you."

Thomas brought the front legs of his chair down with a crash and gave a shout of raucous laughter. "Fairy! That's rich—what a name for a lumbering great brute of a dog!"

"I don't care what she looks like," Harriet's temper was rising fast. "But at least she's well behaved, unlike some people."

"All this fuss about a dog," said Nurse tranquilly. "Silly animals, I say. Give me a nice pussy any day."

"I am with you there, Nurse," said Thomas in his most lordly manner. "But Dr. Jessop wouldn't be. That disgusting muddy creature he brought into the house the other day—you saw the mess it made of Mama's room."

"And the stairs," said James, gloating. "There was mud all over the stairs."

At this point Harriet's temper leaped right out of her control. "Papa didn't take that dog in. He thought it was yours. He thought it was the sort of dog you would have," she shouted, shaking her clenched fist.

"It wouldn't have followed any of us into the house," said Thomas, looking coolly at her furious face. "It would only pick on a dog-lover."

"How do you know what it would pick on?" raged Harriet. "You might as well say that it picked on your house because there were dog-lovers in it."

Thomas ignored this. "But the worst thing was that when your father had got the brute upstairs he let it leap around all over Mama, he didn't make any attempt to control it. He even let it roll on her bed."

Harriet was almost beside herself at the injustice of this version of the episode. "He didn't *let* it," she screamed. "He thought it was your dog, and he had to be careful how he treated it. He thought you were the sort of people to have awful dogs like that."

Thomas looked her up and down with a faint smile. "Oh, dear me, Fallowfield *maxime ferox*. James, you'd better throw some water over her to cool her down."

James leaped up. "Will tea do? I've got some left in my cup."

"You'll do no such thing," said Nurse. "Now you just sit down and behave yourself, and stop teasing the young lady. She isn't used to boys like you."

"Or *sal volatile*, Nurse," Thomas went on. "That's what they give to old ladies with the vapors, isn't it?"

"Mama's got *sal volatile* in her medicine cupboard. She gave it to Cook when Cook saw the mouse. Don't you remember?

Oh, do let me get it!" James was leaping off his chair in his
excitement.

"Now, now, now," said Nurse. "Enough's enough—that's
what I say. Don't you pay any attention to them, dear. They're
just like their papa was when he was a boy. My word, he was a
caution, too." She clicked her tongue.

"Who's Joshua like then? I bet he's not as good as Papa," said
James.

"Master Joshua's like your poor Uncle Edward that died.
Such a nice young gentleman he was."

"I'd rather be like Papa," stated James very emphatically.
"He's much the best person to be like."

Harriet pursed her lips and made a little grimace, which
Thomas unfortunately observed. He was just about to hit back,
when there was the sound of running feet on the stairs, and
Joshua, panting, burst into the room. He had the gray dress
with him, crumpled up and stowed away under his arm, but his
mind was on other matters.

"Papa's terribly angry about something," he said, with consternation all over his face. "I can hear him in the hall."

James shot off his chair and was at the door in an instant. "I
must go and listen, Joshua. Let me through. I bet the undergraduates have been jumping on the hen-house again. Oh, get
out of the way."

"You'll do no such thing, Master James," ordered Nurse.
"I've never heard of anything like it, going to listen to your
papa's private conversation. What are we coming to?"

James, scowling, slunk back to his chair, and kicked his heels
loudly on the legs. Harriet felt very alarmed. If Professor Smith
was being so angry in the hall, how in the world was she going
to get past him, and out of the house?

"Well, it wasn't exactly private," said Joshua. "He was bellowing so. It seemed to be about elephants. I couldn't help
overhearing a bit of it," he said guiltily.

Elephants, thought Harriet with a terrible sinking inside her. Then it must be Aunt Louisa, whom she had totally forgotten.

"If it isn't private, then I'm going to listen," announced James. "Anyway, I bet Joshua hung over the banisters and listened. He's been away for hours. If I just went out on the landing I could hear. I can hear better than anyone else in the house."

"Quiet, James," ordered Thomas ferociously, thumping the small boy down onto his chair again. "Did you say elephants, Joshua?"

"Yes, there's a lady down there with him, only she isn't shouting so loud, so I can't hear. But they seem to be talking about how much an elephant eats in a day. Fancy Papa bothering about that." Joshua's eyes were round with astonishment.

Thomas brought his fist down upon the tablecloth with a bang that made all the cups rattle on their saucers. "It's somebody to do with this girl. All her family are demented about animals. I'm going down to restore her to the bosom of her family."

Harriet hoped frantically that Nurse would put a stop to this. But she merely got up and began to clear away the tea things in a tranquil way.

"I'm coming with you, then," said James. "It's not fair just you going."

"You can go with Master Thomas if you ask them in the kitchen for a nice piece of brown paper to wrap around the young lady's dress. We can't have her going through the streets with it as it is. I don't know what her mama would say. Now ask nicely, Master James, mind. Are your fingers sticky?"

"They're all right," said James impatiently. "Oh, come on, Thomas, or Papa will have finished being angry."

"But he had not. As soon as they were out on the landing they could hear his voice in the hall. James clattered at a great pace down the stairs to get nearer the scene. Thomas, giving a scornful smile over his shoulder to Harriet, followed at a more dignified pace. "It's a pity to get so worked up about animals. They're not worth it."

"It's your papa who seems to be worked up," retorted Harriet angrily.

They caught up with James on the next landing. He was standing leaning gleefully over the banisters and peering down into the hall. They joined him and looked down. Harriet was right about Professor Smith. He appeared to be furiously angry, with a flushed red face, and Aunt Louisa stood with both hands folded on her umbrella handle, watching him with a grim and wintry smile. She held up her hand.

"It did not need all that, sir, to persuade me that you were beyond hope. However," she smoothed out the fingers of her glove, "I am glad to report that there is at least one person of the right way of thinking in your household."

"And who is that, pray?" demanded the professor.

"If I told you that, you would probably savagely attack the person. No, I must decline to reveal it, and hope that the light will spread through the house and perhaps reach even you."

James, now standing on tiptoe and leaning down danger-ously, forgot himself in his excitement. "I bet it's Joshua," he said loudly. "He's always sorry for everything."

Professor Smith strode to the foot of the stairs. "My after-noon's work has already been wrecked, James, and I warn you that I am in a savage mood. If you are wise, you will return this instant to the schoolroom."

"But Nurse sent me down to get some brown paper for this girl," said James in an aggrieved voice.

"I give you exactly three minutes, then, to do so. If you are not out of sight within that time, it will be the worse for you." His father looked grimly at the grandfather clock that stood in the hall.

James shot down the stairs at a tremendous rate, jumped from the third stair up, and clattered off down the hall, calling back over his shoulder, "I couldn't help jumping. You said I'd got to hurry."

"And you too, Thomas," said his father, breathing hard as Thomas came down the stairs. "And who is this small female whose face I seem to know?"

"She's a Miss Jessop. She likes animals too, particularly spotty dogs."

"It appears to be a family failing," said Professor Smith.

All the way down the stairs Harriet had been feverishly wondering what she could do to show her utter scorn and contempt for the Smiths and their rude, blustering ways. And at this point, much to her surprise, inspiration came to her. With a loudness and suddenness that startled her, she shouted: "Jumbo forever!" Then she dodged past Professor Smith, pulled open the front door, darted out, and banged it with the utmost force she could summon.

Chapter 6

"Action, Action, Action"

*B*oth Harriet and Miss Jessop held their heads high on the way home, though they said very little to each other, and certainly did not discuss what had passed in the Smiths' house. Harriet, marching along at a furious rate, her lips pursed, and whirling the unwrapped gray dress as she walked, was thinking that come what might she would fight for Jumbo to the last breath in her body. She was not perfectly clear what it was all about, but she was positive that whatever it was, the Smiths were in the wrong. "It's just their sheer, wicked prejudice," she muttered to herself. It was "sheer, wicked prejudice" that her old nurse had talked about when she was a small girl and had refused to drink milk with skin on it.

Her aunt spoke to her just as they parted company on Bradmore Road. "Do not think that I have been in the least put out by what that overbearing man had to say, Harriet. It has only made me more determined. Besides, there is one of us in the household now."

"One of us?" repeated Harriet doubtfully.

"A follower. We must keep in touch with her—and lose no opportunity of spreading light into the black heart of that man. As I said to him, how are we to expect peace and goodwill in this world while there are people who are indifferent to animals?"

Harriet privately was rather doubtful about the enthusiasm of the maid, if that was the follower Aunt Louisa meant, but one thing she was certain about, and that was the black heart of Professor Smith and his sons, and she felt ready to pledge her every Saturday threepence to fight them tooth and nail, and not to stop until they were cringing in defeat.

Even Dr. Jessop, who usually did not notice much, saw her fierce expression that evening, as she sat by the drawing room fire with an unread book on her lap, looking into the flames.

"Well, who are you plotting to murder, eh, Hetty?" he said, giving her hair a pull. "Your geography teacher?"

She was rather startled at her thoughts being read so easily. "I don't want to murder them exactly, but oh, I'd like to . . ." She ground her teeth, not knowing what she would like to do to them.

"Here, steady on, Hetty, you're getting as bad as your aunt. Only she would plunge a knife into a man and smooth out her gloves with the other hand. Never known a woman be so violent so calmly."

"William," said his wife warningly from the midst of the papers she was studying, and no more was said on the subject then.

Harriet passed her father at the top of the stairs on her way up to bed. "Calmed down yet, Hetty?" he asked.

"Oh, Papa," she burst out, "I do with I could be angry calmly. I always spoil things by being angry angrily."

Her father seemed very taken aback. "Well, why be angry at all? Have you thrown another parcel at those boys?"

"No, but I'd like to. They make me so furious that I just

shout and stamp, and then they laugh. Sometimes I even cry
I'm so angry. I didn't today, but I sometimes do."

Dr. Jessop bellowed with laughter. "You certainly used to
when you were a little girl. My word, I've never seen such a
small creature so eaten up with rage."

"No, but I still do." Harriet held on to the banisters and
kicked them disconsolately. "Those boys called me Fallowfield
Ferox, because I got so angry. Aunt Louisa didn't get angry. I
wish I could be like her."

"Fallowfield Ferox was a master of a dog," said her father
indignantly. "Never been anything to beat him. There's no
harm in being called that."

"Then they called me a most ferocious damsel."

"Oh, I see. Well, don't you go wishing you were like your
Aunt Louisa. You stay as you are, and don't bother your head
with Professor Smith's boys. We've all of us blotted our copy-
books in that household, and we'd better keep away from it."
Dr. Jessop gave a roar of laughter as he thought back again to
the episode of the muddy dog.

There was a sound of feet walking across the tiles in the
gloomy shadows of the hall below, and then the gong boomed
and clashed, startling them both.

"Well," said Dr. Jessop, "that's dinner. I must say I'm ready
for it too—though I suppose it's only mutton hash. I seem to
remember your mother saying something about it when she
stopped me from having any more mutton last night." He
started to go downstairs.

"Papa," Harriet called after him into the shadows. "What are
they doing about Jumbo?"

"Your aunt doesn't want him to go." Dr. Jessop paused and
turned around.

"I know, Papa," she wailed. "But can they stop it?"

"Your aunt and people of her way of thinking are trying to
work up public opinion to stop it—forming societies and such-

like. You'd think they were going to sell the Crown Jewels, all the fuss that's going on."

"But Papa, it is sad."

"So they say. Can't see it myself. Oh, well, forward the mutton hash." And Dr. Jessop disappeared down the staircase. Harriet listened to the dining room door being opened. A streak of light shone into the hall for a moment, and the door was shut.

What she needed, Harriet realized as she walked to school beside Polly the next day, was people on her side. She spent the whole of the morning's lessons looking surreptitiously around the classroom, seeing who might do. There wasn't anybody really suitable, she thought gloomily. They were all so young and silly, and she doubted very much whether they could ever be made serious about anything, even something as important as Jumbo. Besides, she did not know any of them very well. Perhaps there might be some people sitting behind her whom she had overlooked. She tried to glance back over her shoulder to see. It looked, after all, as if it would have to be Agatha.

Agatha was the youngest of five sisters who were all at the school, and Harriet always envied her for the familiar footing that this gave her with the older pupils. Though she was younger than Harriet, Harriet was rather impressed by her grown-up manner. She put it to her at luncheon when they were all eating mince in the dark dining room in the basement.

"Agatha," she said, "did you ever see Jumbo when you went to the Zoological Gardens?"

Agatha was picking her way disdainfully through the cabbage, on the lookout for caterpillars. Harriet was always so hungry that she ate it fast without thinking of such things. Now Agatha put down her fork and wrinkled her nose in a disgusted way.

"I should think Miss Raby goes down to the market herself

every day and picks out all the most horrible cabbages. Yes, I
did see Jumbo. And Alice too."

"Who's Alice?"

"His wife. Didn't you go to see her too? What could you have
been about?"

"There wasn't much time left after I had been for a ride on
Jumbo," said Harriet defensively.

"Oh, did you go for a ride?" Agatha was scornful. "Mary and
Clementine said only children did that."

For once Harriet paid no attention to this grown-up air. "I
didn't know there was Alice too. That makes it much worse."

"Oh, I don't suppose he'll go to America, if that's what you
mean," said Agatha with great confidence. "Papa says public
opinion would never stand for it."

"The *Morning Post* says they are already making the box that
he's to go in," said Harriet with a touch of triumph at being
one up on Agatha's papa. Agatha was shaken by this.

"How cruel they are! Just think of the poor thing being made
to leave Alice. Why, the keeper said they were so fond of each
other that they used to twine their trunks around each other."

"My aunt's working to stop them from sending Jumbo to
America," said Harriet very fast, afraid that Agatha might
interrupt before she heard the whole of it. "We're trying to get
money to buy him ourselves if the Zoological Gardens say that
he's got to be sold." This was invention; Harriet did not really
know what her aunt's schemes were, but she felt she must put a
target in front of Agatha, if she was to be persuaded to join in.

"What would we do with him if we did buy him?" Agatha
had an exceedingly practical mind. "One of our maids won a
pig in a raffle once, and it was a terrible nuisance trying to give
him away."

"Oh, I expect Aunt Louisa would arrange something," said
Harriet vaguely. "But anyway, we've got to raise masses of
money to help feed him, and push leaflets through people's

doors to ask them to contribute—there's heaps to be done, and we need as many people as possible."

"I've got a shilling," said Agatha unexpectedly. "You can have that, and if you like I'll ask Mary and Clementine. I don't know about pushing things through people's doors, though. I'm sure Mama wouldn't like it."

"My Aunt Louisa does it." But Harriet was too jubilant about her unexpected follower to press the matter further. Besides, she could lead up to it gradually.

She reported her success very excitedly to Aunt Louisa after school that day.

"One, Harriet?" said her aunt coolly. "But it is thousands that we need. Thousands of children to march upon London and demonstrate outside the Gardens, thousands of adult animal-lovers to subscribe to our funds. We have an enormous task before us. There is the petition that we are going to present to Parliament too; we want a million names on that."

"But there aren't a thousand girls in the school," said Harriet, hurt. "Not two hundred, even."

"And if there were, we could not count on all of them—such is the small-mindedness of the general run of mankind. No, what we must try to do is to tap every single household in Oxford, and out of those perhaps we can form a nucleus of valiant hearts who will tread our way with us. That can be your duty, Harriet."

"Every single house in Oxford!" said Harriet, appalled. "But I haven't even seen all of Oxford."

"Never mind, there is a beginning to all things. And you have your friend Agatha."

Harriet thought about the matter that evening. Sometimes it seemed easy, something one could undertake on a Saturday; after all, you had only to walk down every street in Oxford, and there couldn't be as many as all that. It need only be half the streets in Oxford, since there was Agatha. Then a sense of the hundreds, the thousands of houses that there were on the way to school alone would come over her, and the task would become like a nightmare. But still, it was an excitement to have at last a cause that one really felt passionately about. The best thing of all about the Jumbo cause was that nobody could ask her to make over her dresses into coats and comforters for elephants. Giggling a little at the thought, she fell asleep.

Miss Jessop was waiting outside the school when Harriet came out the following afternoon.

"Alone, Harriet?" she said. "But where is your young friend?"

"Oh, are we going to start today, then?" Harriet said blankly.

Her aunt pointed grimly to two canvas knapsacks at her feet; they were crammed with leaflets. "Action, action, action. I thought you understood the need for that, Harriet."

Harriet looked around hopelessly. She knew how immovable her aunt was; very likely she would make Harriet carry both knapsacks. There was a knot of girls from the second class standing talking by the school door with their heads close together. Agatha was sure to be there. Nobody was fonder of talking than she was. Harriet ran up.

"Agatha," she said breathlessly, "can you start today? With Jumbo, I mean. My aunt's here. Please come," she begged.

Miss Jessop had picked up the knapsacks by the time Harriet had dragged Agatha up to her. "Good afternoon," she said briskly. "Welcome to our little band. Here is your afternoon's task." She thrust the knapsack at the child. "I can accompany you as far as St. Giles Church, and there I must leave you."

Agatha was gaping, with a dropped jaw and an alarmed expression. "But what about tea? Mama will be expecting me to tea."

"Tea?" said Miss Jessop scornfully. "What is tea to us? Think of Jumbo's tea, Agatha—poor, suffering dumb animal."

Agatha was silenced. More than ever Harriet admired her aunt, and wished she could override people's objections like this, especially those of Agatha, who ordinarily could go on arguing for an hour.

"But I'll have to tell one of the others to let Mama know I'm going to be late," wailed Agatha at Miss Jessop's departing back. It was Harriet, however, who spotted Clementine and told her, and then both girls set off after Miss Jessop at a run.

It was difficult to catch up with her; she was striding at such a rate, and the canvas bags, awkward to carry, bumped and jolted against their knees. When they finally appeared, one on each side of her, Miss Jessop looked at them with surprise.

"What, have you dealt with this road already?" she asked. Harriet looked back blankly. "Houses, houses, houses," said Miss Jessop impatiently. "All about us are houses. And you are leaving them in the darkness of their ignorance. Action, action," she repeated. "One of you ought to be on each side of the road, distributing these as fast as is within your powers. You are bringing light into darkness, remember, and saving an innocent animal untold suffering."

Agatha looked frightened and a little rebellious. Harriet hesitated and then plunged boldly down the path and up the steps of the nearest house, not without a sense that she was trespassing, and was being covertly watched by unseen eyes behind the lace curtains in the front room. Then, with a proud sense of duty being done and the first step taken, she walked down again, and up the path of the next house. Aunt Louisa watched impatiently.

"Harriet, Harriet, what time you waste. You are not paying a formal call." Harriet stood in the middle of the path, looking bewildered. "Step over the wall, child," called Miss Jessop, indicating the nine-inch parapet that separated the two front-door steps.

Harriet pushed her leaflet through the letter box and scurried back. "But isn't it taking liberties, Aunt Louisa?" she said in a low voice.

"Liberties? Stuff and nonsense. Why, I have scrambled over an iron paling before now, *and* hit a cabman over the head with my umbrella. One has to be ruthless, Harriet, ruthless in the pursuit of an ideal."

"Whatever happened to the cabman?" said Harriet, aghast.

"The umbrella broke," said Miss Jessop shortly.

There was a long garden wall after this, and then some stables, and thus no letter boxes, Harriet thankfully observed. But at the next house Miss Jessop stopped. "And here I must leave you," she said briskly. "I have work to do at my committee rooms." She waved her hand in the direction of the front door, which stood a little way open. Pinned on to it was a rather crumpled piece of paper. "Jumbo Defense League" was printed in untidy capitals in red ink that had blurred with the rain. A clumsy drawing of a hand pointed one finger through into the hall.

"We are not without helpers, even in Oxford." Then Miss Jessop dived into her reticule. "I forgot. you are still without your badges." Out of the depths of her reticule she produced two bits of red ribbon. Stuck on to the middle of each was a scrap of lined paper which looked as though it had been torn from an exercise book, with a crayoned drawing on it, just recognizable as the head of an elephant. There was a large bent pin by which you could attach it to your coat. "Come now, don't dawdle; pin them on," said Miss Jessop as the girls looked at them rather doubtfully. "Then you can bear yourselves with pride as friends of our beloved elephant."

It was difficult to pin them on; the paper was inclined to tear, and the ribbon to flop down and hide the drawings. But Miss Jessop had not the time to pay attention to this sort of detail. "And now I leave you. Should you want further supplies of leaflets, you will find me here. And please leave your empty knapsacks on the step when you have finished."

The girls watched her upright gray back disappear through the door.

"But there are thousands," said Agatha in horror, plunging her hands among the leaflets. "And the bag's so heavy—we'll never be able to carry them far."

"Come on, then," said Harriet. "Let's push them through the doors. We'll have a race if you like; you do one side of the road, and I'll do the other." She felt eager and full of enthusiasm, and ahead of her was a row of houses with street doors conveniently near each other.

But Agatha hung back, looking at the bulging knapsack with distaste. "I don't think we ought to, Harriet. I don't think it's proper, and I'm sure Mama wouldn't either. And supposing somebody saw us from the school. We might even see Miss Raby."

"We could say my aunt sent us to do charity work."

"Yes, but your aunt . . ." Agatha hesitated, and then said with a rush, "Well, I don't think she's a very proper person. I mean, she hit a cabman, she said so herself."

"I expect it was only because he was unkind to his horse," said Harriet impatiently. "Oh, do come on, otherwise it will be time to go home before we have done anything."

Without giving Agatha a chance to argue more, she set off at a run. She looked over her shoulder as she went up the steps of the first house; Agatha still had not crossed the road. So Harriet, when she had dealt with that house, crossed the road herself. Agatha lingered near the gate of the second house, and then rather dispiritedly pushed open the gate and mounted the steps. Harriet, keeping her eye anxiously on the other side of the road, continued down her side. Agatha followed on her side, but slowly, and Harriet soon outstripped her, though the canvas bag seemed no lighter. In this fashion they proceeded down the broad street of St. Giles, until Harriet reached the building that her father had told her was Balliol College, and judged she could do no good there. She crossed the street again and waited for Agatha. As she watched the girl slowly and reluctantly making her way toward her, she felt very low. Agatha was really precious little use as an ally. She herself could have enjoyed the whole affair, but it was all spoiled by having to drag Agatha around with her, watching her nervously in case she decided to throw in her hand. It was always the same in any of her schemes: they were spoiled by the other people who took part in them. Why couldn't she for once find somebody who would join in wholeheartedly?

But when Agatha came up at last, her bag seemed emptier than Harriet's. "How ever did you do it?" Harriet said in amazed envy. She looked back along Agatha's side of St. Giles, but there seemed to be no more houses there than on the other side. Agatha seemed uncomfortable and rubbed the toe of her shoe around the flagstone where she stood.

"You haven't been putting more than one leaflet in each door!" said Harriet incredulously.

Agatha defended herself with heat. "Well, I don't know how many people are living in each house, do I? Some of them might even be colleges with hundreds of people. Anyway, we must do something; otherwise we'll never empty these horrible bags. I ought to be going home now, in fact. Harriet, let's go home."

"We can't," said Harriet dully. "We've hardly done anything yet."

"Yes, we have. Look how long this street is. And I'm so tired."

Harriet spoke with great despair and determination. "Look, we've *got* to do a bit more. We can rest a little if you like, but then we must do this street." She indicated Beaumount Street on her right. "The houses are beautifully near each other, and there aren't even any paths up to the doors."

Agatha made a sulky mouth and said nothing. Both girls

stood aimlessly on the pavement under the dull March sky. A sharp wind blew against them, and seemed to penetrate every layer of clothing. People hurried past them, bending their heads to the wind, and holding their hats.

"We can't stay here," said Agatha suddenly. "Everybody can see us, and we must look so odd, just standing here by ourselves. Somebody is sure to recognize us and tell Miss Raby."

"Let's go down here then," said Harriet, crossly, pointing to Beaumont Street. She wondered how much longer she would keep her temper under control. How marvelous it must be to be a general, she thought. They just have to command, and they were obeyed; none of this shilly-shallying from people with objections. "We could start pushing these things through the doors here," she said aloud. She could see the brass of the letter boxes gleaming in an inviting line all the way down the street. How tempting they looked. Agatha followed her around the corner.

"But I'm so tired," she said dolefully, "and my arm aches so."

"Well, sit down on the pavement then," Harriet snapped at her, her temper breaking out at last. It startled Agatha, who gave her a frightened sideways glance, and said nothing more. They went around the corner into Beaumont Street, and leaned up against a wall there. They did not look at each other, but stared straight in front of them, both a little ashamed.

"I wonder what the leaflets say," said Harriet in a voice that she hoped was unconcerned. "I haven't looked yet."

She pulled one of them out of her bag and smoothed it open. It was printed on poor quality paper in very black letters, a little smudged here and there, and with many exclamation marks. There was a rather rough drawing of an elephant at the top, with tears rolling down its trunk. "JUMBO—A SLAVE?" was the heading.

Agatha looked over Harriet's shoulder to read it, forgetting that she had some hundreds of copies in her own bag. " 'The

Americans are notorious for their cruel and wicked habits of slavery,' " she read out. " 'Is it to this nation of savage barbarians that we shall sell our beloved Jumbo?' Goodness, Harriet, I didn't know that Americans were like that."

"You see," said Harriet triumphantly. "And you won't even push these things through people's doors to save him."

" 'This innocent, trusting animal looks to YOU to be saved!!!' " Agatha picked out another paragraph. " 'Can you stay stony-hearted in the face of his appeal? Dip your hands deep in your pockets, deeper still. Remember, you are an Englishman! And it is to England that all the world looks for leadership!!!' Oh, Harriet, there's my shilling, I'd forgotten. I'll give it to you at school tomorrow."

"Hallo, here's Fallowfield Ferox," said a boy's voice.

The two girls, absorbed in the leaflet, and forgetting their surroundings, gave a huge start and looked up. Thomas, Joshua, and James were advancing upon them up Beaumont Street.

"I'm sorry you haven't got a parcel to throw this time," said Thomas from a distance of several yards. "But won't those do as well?" He pointed to the knapsacks.

"She's getting really cross now," said James, peering at Harriet with satisfaction. "I can tell by the way her nose goes in and out," he added in a loud whisper to Joshua. "No, Joshua, don't pinch. She can't hear."

Thomas strolled up to them in a lordly way. "And how is all the menagerie?" Then he peered at their badges. Harriet clapped her hand in a shamefaced way over hers, but it was too late. "It's an elephant!" he shouted in triumphant amusement. "They've got drawings of elephants pinned on them, Fallowfield Ferox and her little friend. It must be that stupid Jumbo that everybody's going mad about."

James rushed up. "Why have they got drawings pinned on to them? Oh, do let me see."

"Just because they're so obsessed about animals. Animals before human beings, Papa said."

Harriet was losing control of her temper again. "I'd rather have any animal than you." She searched her mind furiously for an animal low enough. "Even a beetle."

"Ooh, Fallowfield *maxime ferox*, isn't she, Thomas?"

There was no knowing to what lengths Harriet might not have gone under all these taunts, but two things happened. A small, rather cross-looking man came hurrying up the street, clearly in pursuit of the boys. The other thing, which happened at the same instant, was that Agatha suddenly broke into song. Harriet had forgotten about her for the moment in her rage and excitement, but Agatha stepped forward, and brandishing her knapsack, started singing in a loud voice, a little out of tune, but very powerfully:

> *"Jumbo said to Alice, 'I love you,'*
> *Alice said to Jumbo, 'I don't believe you do,*
> *For if you really loved me, as you say you do*
> *You wouldn't go to Yankee land and leave me at the*
> *zoo!' "*

Then she thrust her hand into the canvas bag, took out a handful of leaflets, flung them in the faces of the astounded boys, tipped up the bag so that the rest were emptied over their feet, and rushed off down the street.

Chapter 7

The Smiths' Counterattack

*I*t was a far more striking gesture, Harriet had to admit, than her own throwing of the parcel. That had been just bad temper, which had shamed her more than anyone else. But this was a masterstroke of Agatha's. There the boys had stood in a flood of leaflets that eddied around their ankles, papers whirling in the stiff March wind, and bowling down the street—Harriet had seen it all in the split second before she too took to her heels. She allowed herself one further glance back when they got to the bottom of Beaumont Street and were just about to turn into Walton Street. There, at the top of the street, were the crouching figures of the boys, picking up the leaflets, while the man who seemed to be in charge of them stamped angrily up and down. And Agatha, of course, had an empty knapsack to hand in at the committee rooms, while Harriet's was still two-thirds full, in spite of her thrusting leaflets in the letter boxes all the way up Walton Street.

The next day was Saturday, and so there was no chance of discussing the matter further with Agatha, nor of hearing what her four elder sisters had said about it all. Nor was there any Aunt Louisa or any walk today. Saturdays were very dull altogether. Harriet sat in the dining room with her mother, who was cutting out calico chemises on the table. Harriet was supposed to run tacking threads through them, so that the Female Prisoners could stitch them, however little they knew about dressmaking. It was coarse, stiff stuff, and her fingers felt sore with the effort of pushing the needle through. She pitied the Female Prisoners having to struggle with the hems and the buttonholes, but then, looking at the pile which still needed tacking, pitied herself more—the Prisoners would only have to do one each, and, after all, it was for themselves.

Outside, the wind blew in sudden gusts, and rain rattled against the panes. Gray clouds rushed across the sky, and such trees as she could see looked black and hopeless; it was impossible to believe that they could ever bear green leaves, or to imagine what they would look like if they did. Her mother's scissors ground away at the calico. Then she looked up suddenly, after a long silence, her scissors still poised with their jaws open.

"Oh, Harriet, I forgot to say. I had a note this morning from Miss Edale. She says that she feels herself to be better, and hopes to resume her walks with you on Monday. So I have told your aunt that she need not give up any more of her valuable time." She gave Harriet a sharp look. "I think it is probably just as well because you seem to have been very overexcited the past week or so. Your aunt has not been trying to interest you in the cabmen's horses, has she? She is inclined to be a little unbalanced on the subject, and it is a cause really not worth overexciting yourself about."

"I don't think she has mentioned horses lately, Mama."

Harriet had a moment of anxiety, wondering whether her mother was going to ask about Jumbo, but Mrs. Jessop had forgotten, it seemed, her sister-in-law's violence on the subject.

She bent low over the table, facing the window to make the most of the light. It took the light from Harriet, and she let the calico that she was stitching fall into her lap. A pencil and paper lay near her, on which her mother had been keeping a record of the number of garments cut out, and she picked them up idly, and without thinking started scribbling. At first she just tried to see how faultlessly she could write her name in copperplate. Then she wrote Agatha's. "Agatha Mortlake," she inscribed, and underneath it. "Our Side." Then to balance it she wrote on the other side, "T., J., and J. Smith—the Enemies." She underlined it heavily, and bit the pencil hard until the top splintered and left bits of wood in her mouth. It was as she was picking the wood off the lead of the pencil that it occurred to her to use that bit of paper for marking victories and defeats. Under "Our Side" she immediately put "Agatha's knapsack—victory," and then, after a little hesitation, "My parcel." She was going to mark it as a victory, but then she remembered the humiliation that had followed, and thinking of the list of history dates they used at school, full of battles like those of the Civil War, she added after it, "Indecisive." The Enemies, on the other hand, did not seem to have scored any notable victories, but feeling she ought to be scrupulously fair if the list was to be any good, she wrote, "Fallowfield Ferox—minor victory." The list really looked rather important now; it was a pity there was not more to put on it.

"How is the tacking, Harriet?" asked her mother, turning suddenly. "You really should have finished that chemise now." She straightened her back with a jerk, and frowned down on the chemise she was trying to squeeze out of material that inconveniently was just an inch too narrow at the vital point. Harriet gave a jump, and began tacking hastily, the paper thrust under the pile of chemises beside her. It was then that the noise in the street began. At first she thought it was just the ostler's children from the nearby mews playing around

outside the house. But after a minute or so she recognized it as
singing, and in the background a weird music. Her mother took
no notice. Harriet sat with her sewing dropped in her lap,
eyeing the window with increasing impatience. Surely her mother
could just glance out and tell her what it was that was going on
out there. Then she could bear it no longer.

"Who is singing like that out there, Mama?"

"Just boys," said her mother, looking quickly over her shoulder, without any interest. "Really, Harriet, it is pitiful how
easily you are distracted. You ought to be used enough to street
music by now."

But this street music was different. As Harriet took up her
sewing again she picked out some of the words. "Love me, love
my brother, dog says to dog" seemed to be one line, repeated in
a mournful chant, with the droning music behind. Then the
singers started stamping in time, and it was impossible to pick
out any more.

"Oh, Mama, couldn't I just look and see them?" she begged.

Her mother sighed. "Very well, Harriet, but it is time, as I
am always telling you, that you did try to start controlling your
curiosity."

Harriet scrambled to the window, falling over an uncut bale
of calico as she did so. She saw three figures on the pavement
outside the front garden, and pulled aside the lace curtains to
observe them better. The three figures saw her and shouted. It
was the Smiths.

Harriet dropped the curtain as if it had been on fire. Outside,
the shouting was noisier than ever, and Harriet could hear the
chanting of "Love me, love my brother," again. Mrs. Jessop
looked up with a frown.

"Oh, dear, what a terrible noise they are making. Why,
Harriet, you didn't let them see you, did you? Really, for a girl
of nearly twelve you have got very little sense indeed. Now you
will have to go out and give them some money."

This was truly terrible. "Oh, no, Mama, please," said Harriet in an anguished voice.

"We can't have this going on." Mrs. Jessop drew aside the curtains, rapped on the window, and shook her fist sternly at the Smiths. "They're right outside our gate, too."

"I expect they'll go away soon," said Harriet weakly.

"Of course they won't, until they've had their penny." Her mother went to the little tin that stood on the mantelpiece and was labeled "Sundry Charities" in red ink, and took out three ha' pennies. "There you are, give them one each, and tell them to go away at once. Right out of this road."

"But Mama, I can't!" Harriet was in agony now.

Her mother took no notice, but went on pinning and cutting. Harriet walked slowly to the door, and then looked over her shoulder to see if there was any hope of reprieve; her mother did not look up. She walked down the hall, hoping that if she did it slowly enough the noise would have stopped by the time she reached the street door. But the shouts seemed to get louder and more impatient. When she at last opened the door there was a howl of cheering.

"Now then, all together," roared Thomas, waving his arms like a bandmaster, while Joshua in the background blew away at something that Harriet recognized as a comb and paper. The two others leaned over the garden gate and shouted:

> *"Love me, love my brother,*
>   *Dog sings to dog.*
> *Let's all love each other*
>   *Frog sings to frog.*
> *If the world weren't so wide*
>   *Pig sings to pig,*
> *I'd lie down by your side.*
>   *But the world's too big."*

They followed it up by stamping and cheering, and James climbed up on the garden gate and rattled a tin at her. There was a sound of sharp rapping on the dining room window, and Mrs. Jessop could be seen standing there, with a very severe expression. James jumped down again. Harriet rushed down the path toward them.

"She's got money for us," shrieked James. "How much do you think it'll be, Thomas?"

"We can't take money," Harriet heard Joshua saying in a horrified voice.

"You've got to take the money," Harriet said with fury, and hoping that this would humiliate them for the rest of their days, she seized the tin from James and pushed in the ha' pennies. "It comes from the Sundry Charities tin," she added vindictively, just to rub it in a little more. "We usually give it to tramps."

Joshua went scarlet with embarrassment and confusion at being given money as though he were a street Arab. If Thomas was humiliated, he concealed it well. "Thank you kindly, Lady, I'm sure," he said in a mocking way, acting the part of a street Arab and pulling his forelock. (But it probably was to hide his real feelings, Harriet thought.) James, however, was just elated by the prospect of extra pocket money, and peered greedily into his tin, which was labeled, Harriet had time to notice, "Smiths' Defense Fund." There was another sharp tattoo of raps on the window. Mrs. Jessop was now shaking her cutting-out scissors warningly at the boys. Joshua turned and fled, and the other two followed him, though more slowly, turning around to grin derisively over their shoulders. Harriet stood there, paying no attention to the rain, and watched them in their long ulsters, disappearing around the corner. Her heart was pounding with fury, and she clenched and unclenched her fist.

When she got back to the dining room her mother was putting away her scissors and pins in the round mahogany sewing table. "I have to go out now, Harriet," she said. "Some-

body must see Thrupp's about the inferior brand of cotton they
are supplying to the Prisoners' Needlework Guild, and I suppose
it must be I. I must leave you to give tea to your papa when he
comes in. I'll tell Polly to bring the tea tray at half past four. I
have left quite enough tacking to keep you busy."

As soon as her mother had left the room Harriet fumbled for
her list of battles. She stared at it for a minute or so, and then
on the enemy side she wrote: "Singing an impertinent song—
victory." After this she was far too angry to sit still, but paced
the dining room, muttering hatred to herself. It was not just
herself the boys were hitting at this time; she was quite sure it
was her father too, with his saying, "Love me, love my dog,"
and probably her aunt as well.

Her mother went out of the house, and the front door
slammed behind her. Harriet crossed to the window and drummed
her fingers furiously. The sound of her mother's steps faded into
the distance, and there was silence. She did not hear the sound
of footsteps approaching; she was too deep in thoughts about
the Smiths, and she was completely taken by surprise when the
figure of her aunt appeared at the gate. It took Polly some time
to answer the front door; she had probably been deep in her
afternoon "bit of feet up." "There's only Miss Harriet who's in,
miss," Harriet heard her say doubtfully.

"Miss Harriet will do," her aunt said briskly, and then she
marched into the dining room. "Victory, Harriet, we have
scored a notable victory!"

Harriet turned eagerly from the window,, hoping that perhaps her aunt might have come to tell her of a crushing defeat
of the Smiths, some disaster as they were running triumphantly
from Bradmore Road. "Is it the boys?" she said excitedly.

"Boys, boys? What boys?" Her aunt frowned a moment. "No,
Harriet. It is Jumbo—a reprieve!" She waved a piece of paper as
she spoke.

"In that bit of paper?" said Harriet, bewildered, trying to

remember what had happened in *The Rose and the Ring* when
Prince Gigolo had been reprieved.

"An injunction from Mr. Justice Chitty," said her aunt
slowly and solemnly, "forbidding Jumbo's departure until further inquiries have been made."

Harriet felt ashamed. The truth was that she had been so
wrapped up in her private war with the Smiths, she had quite
forgotten about the cause she was supporting. "Oh, Aunt Louisa, I am glad," she said loudly, trying to whip herself up into
great enthusiasm. "Will he always stay in the Zoological Gardens now?"

Miss Jessop held up a warning finger. "Harriet, Harriet, so
like your father, always blindly optimistic! No, it is by no means
certain that we have won our battle—I should say that much
blood remains to be shed. But we have been granted a few days'
respite; the law of England is on our side! But we cannot afford
to lay down our arms. What we must do now is to keep people
in touch with developments. See." She flung down on the table
a bundle of leaflets. "I have had this bulletin printed, and it is
now for you and me to distribute them."

Harriet picked one up. The ink was still wet, and she smudged
it. Miss Jessop however did not seem at all put out by the black
fingerprints all over the page. "Wet from the printing press,"
she said with relish. "I stood over that man with my umbrella
raised and told him that unless I had them by three o'clock I
would strike. He produced them—they always do if only one is
determined enough."

The leaflets looked as though they had been printed by
someone who was watching out of the corner of an eye in case
the umbrella struck. The type was crooked on the page; the
punctuation was rather odd; and there were a good many
spelling mistakes. "MR. JUSTICE CHITTY OUR SAVIUR!" it
was headed. And underneath: "Ley all animal loversoffer thanks
to the mighty justice of England this day which has protected

an innocen animal from those rapacious, men who wish to sell him for filthy!! lucre Supporters of the Jumbo Defense League that is what your aid has achieved! Donotslacken your endeavors but give and give and give Agin."

"Come, Harriet," said her aunt. "Hurry, there is much to do. Your coat, quickly."

"But what are we going to do?" asked Harriet, as she hurried down the garden path beside her aunt, still buttoning up her coat. "And I did tell Mama I would give Papa his tea."

"Then your father must, for once, give up his tea. He is too much a slave to such habits, brutish habits, I might say."

"But what are we going to do?" Harriet asked again after a few minutes' silence, as they turned onto the Banbury road.

"We are going to distribute this bulletin throughout the University. Some are for us; some are against us. It is of vital importance that we fan the flame of the first, and trample down the resistance of the second."

They marched down St. Giles as though they were a conquering army, pushing the bulletins through the letter boxes as they went. Miss Jessop hammered on each door as she went, but Harriet was not bold enough for this. Aunt Louisa even marched into Balliol College and handed a bundle of bulletins to the porter there, "For distribution to your young gentlemen." She did the same at three other colleges, and then turned onto Canterbury Lane. "We are now going to attack the most diabolical of all our opponents," she said with a ferocious smile over her shoulder to Harriet. "Professor Smith himself."

Trembling with excitement, Harriet trotted after her. She did not know whether she hoped to see the boys or not; she felt that they would get the better of her in any exchange of words—how could she stay calm, for instance, if James shouted out that he could tell by her nose that she was getting angry! On the other hand, there was always the hope that Aunt Louisa could somehow squash them. But Canterbury Lane was empty even of undergraduates. The rawness and the rain had driven them all indoors. The wind blew a dirty piece of paper in front of them as they hurried down the street.

"First a leaflet for the Lodgings," said Aunt Louisa. "We must not neglect the high places." She handed Harriet one to push through the letter box, and as she was putting it in, the sound of a dreary wailing came drifting down from an upper-story window of the next house, the Smiths' house. Aunt Louisa stiffened at once.

"Cats," she said dramatically.

"I don't think so," said Harriet doubtfully. Indeed it sounded to her more like the noise Joshua had been making with his comb.

"It is not the sort of sound that I would expect you to recognize," said Aunt Louisa decisively. "It is the sound of a cat in pain." Her face took on an expression of great sternness. "And knowing whose household this is, I am not surprised to hear it. I have no doubt at all that this professor whatever-his-name-is is tormenting some helpless animal so that he can prove some foolish theory." Taking no notice of Harriet's "Oh, but Aunt Louisa . . ." she hammered the Smiths' door knocker thunderously.

Harriet, alarmed, scuffled several paces back. She did not really want to seem to be in her aunt's company at this point. Her retreat brought the second-floor windows into her view, and there stood James by a window that was open in spite of the weather. He was blowing loudly and untunefully on a comb.

Below, there was a sudden shriek. Harriet looked hastily toward her aunt, and saw the door open and the parlormaid running at full speed away from it, her streamers flying, her shoes slipping on the marble floor. Aunt Louisa turned around.

"The girl seems to be an idiot," she said severely. "But I shall have to wait for somebody more responsible to come. The issue is too serious to be abandoned."

She did not have long to wait. Professor Smith came striding over the hall with such an expression of fury on his face that Harriet hastily moved several yards up the street. Aunt Louisa, however, gave him no time to speak. She pointed up coolly toward the wailing noise.

"May I inquire what sort of cruel experiment you are performing on that wretched animal up there?"

Professor Smith bared his teeth so that he looked like a tiger about to devour its prey. "Madam, it may interest you to learn that in this household we perform cruel experiments only upon human beings." For one terrifying second Harriet really thought he was going to drag them both in for his cruel experiments. But then the door slammed shut.

Chapter 8

A New Recruit

*H*arriet was not at all sure how this exchange between Professor Smith and her aunt should be scored in her list of battles. Her aunt did not seem in the least crushed, but on the other hand there was no denying that Professor Smith had had the last word.

"Are you going to tell the police?" Harriet asked anxiously as they walked back up Canterbury Lane.

"About what, Harriet?"

"That Professor Smith experiments on human beings?"

"I am only concerned with the welfare of animals. If the Professor chooses to vent his cruelty on human beings, that is his own affair; human beings can look after themselves. Though I am inclined to doubt whether he was telling the truth. Men such as he are too cowardly to take on humans—they content themselves with the poor suffering dumb animals."

So Harriet marked it down as "indecisive." But the news about the judge forbidding Jumbo to leave the country—that was a major victory.

That afternoon was the last that Harriet was to spend with
her aunt. On Monday Miss Edale would return and they would
go back to the old routine, and though there was more peace
and security in this, Harriet did feel rather flat at the thought of
it. Her aunt left her with sheaves of pamphlets to distribute
throughout Oxford, and instructions about keeping the inspiration of Jumbo aflame in her heart. "What an example the
patient endurance of that beast sets us, Harriet," she said. "No
sacrifice is too great for us to make for him. Remember that
during the coming week, and dedicate yourself to his cause. I
shall be coming to tea with your mother next Saturday, and
shall hope to hear of thousands of new recruits, thousands of
households behind us."

Inspired by this rousing speech of her aunt's, and conscious of
how difficult it was going to be to do anything about it, Harriet
felt only wrath and despair at school on Monday when Agatha
announced that she was devoting all her time henceforth to
constructing a banner for the Jumbo Defense League.

"Whatever is the good of that?" Harriet asked angrily.

"It will show people who we are and make them look at us.
It's very nice. I've traced a picture from a Natural History we've
got at home, and cut it out from Mama's old gray silk and I'm
going to put a red harness on."

"Elephants don't wear harnesses," said Harriet furiously. She
felt this remark was rather tame, but she wanted to show her
disapproval somehow.

"How do you know they don't? They must. People ride on
them, don't they?"

"They steer them with their feet or with a stick or something."

"Don't be so silly, Harriet. You can't steer anything as big as
an elephant with your feet. Anyway, I don't care. I just want to
make the gray silk stand out more. Mama's let me have an old
white tablecloth, and when they march on London, as your
aunt says they're going to do, they can wave it as they go."

"If you spend all your time sewing, there won't be any people to wave it," said Harriet with passion. "What we want is action."

"Well, I think your sort of action is silly—pushing things through people's mailboxes! How do you know whether they read them or not, anyway? With a banner you'll know that they see that. And if you think I'm going out wearing one of those silly badges again, you're wrong. I could have made better ones when I was six."

Harriet again felt full of helpless rage at the way her only follower was resisting her leadership. She thought again how marvelous it would be if you were a general; you could just shoot people who behaved like this. All through school that day she brooded on the wretchedness of everything. There she was, alone, left to bear the burden of rallying Oxford around her. She had not one single follower whom she could rely upon. She looked stormily around the classroom.

"Have you finished your sum, Harriet?" the teacher asked her. "If not, kindly apply yourself. Remember what Miss Raby said about concentration only this morning in prayers."

As she turned her head back toward her exercise book, with its blur of dirty pencil marks and crossed-out figures, her eyes fell on Agatha, who, with rapt concentration, was making sketches of elephants on her blotting paper. She would like to have had her court-martialed and shot. After school was over, Agatha, who was usually the last to leave because she was so fond of talking, dashed out of the cloakroom door with all her outdoor clothes on as Harriet came walking down the corridor from the classroom. She was obviously determined to waste no time before getting back to sew her banner.

"Traitor," said Harriet under her breath.

Agatha stopped. "What did you say?"

"Nothing," said Harriet airily.

"Yes you did. You said I was a traitor. Well, I'm not, so

there. I'm just as interested as you are. I've spent hours and hours on this banner—you ask Mary or Clementine."

"It's needlework you're interested in," said Harriet scornfully. "Not Jumbo. How can sewing keep him alive?"

"How can pushing things through letter boxes? Anyway, Harriet, don't be so silly. You told me yourself that there was a new law stopping Jumbo from going to America, so why do you want to bother other people about him now?"

"Why do you want to make a banner, then?" Harriet asked furiously.

But Agatha had gone, the door slammed back behind her, so hard that the glass panes rattled. A minute or two later Harriet went out by the same door, slamming it even more furiously, and the glass sounded as though it would break. She carried some of Aunt Louisa's leaflets under one arm; Agatha's behavior had made her more determined than ever. Jumbo might be safe for the time being, but, as Aunt Louisa had said, who knew for how long? Besides, she felt the situation was desperate—herself the only supporter. You couldn't have a children's crusade, surely, with only one person to march in it.

Miss Edale was waiting by the gate. She was heavily muffled and wrapped, and was even wearing a veil. She greeted Harriet with so much warmth that Harriet felt ashamed.

"Now where are we to walk today? I think you must be allowed to choose your favorite walk since you have been so long deprived of them by my ill-health. Still, I am happy to say I feel fully restored now. There is just my neuralgia; that is why I am wearing a veil. Now, Harriet, where is it to be?"

Harriet chose the Botanical Gardens because they lay right at the far end of the town, which would give her an opportunity of distributing most of her leaflets on the way. Besides, she loved the walk down the winding High Street, with its splendor of college buildings on either side. There were open doors too in their massive gates, which gave tantalizing glimpses of even more beautiful buildings beyond, set around stone courtyards, or grassy gardens. Her walks since Miss Edale's illness had mostly been through the redbrick suburb of North Oxford and she was heartily sick of its ugliness.

They walked briskly down Cornmarket Street and turned left into the High Street, where their progress was made slower by the crowded pavements. Harriet peered at everything as she passed, through the gates of the colleges, into the windows of bookshops, up the little cobbled streets, and thought how nice it would be to linger and look for as long as one liked. They followed the High Street down to the bottom of the town, to where the shops came to an end, and there stood, uncrowded by other buildings, what Harriet thought was the most beautiful college of all, with a tower that was crowned with the most delicate little pinnacles, and one wall that was lapped by the river itself. They hesitated on the pavement before crossing the road to the Botanical Gardens, and Harriet looked back at that wall, stained green by the river, and wondered if there was great competition among the people who lived in the college to have a room on that side, so that you could lean out of the window and almost dabble your fingers in the water. She said something of the sort to Miss Edale, who was waiting for a huge brewer's dray to pass before she ventured to cross, although the dray was fully forty yards away and moving very ponderously and slowly. Miss Edale glanced back at the college, and shivered a little.

"Oh, no, Harriet," she said, "I think it would be *most* unpleasant to live on that side. Just think how damp it would be, and there might even be rats. There now, I think we can cross at last."

The Botanical Gardens looked like a private house. There was a garden approach with grass and a graveled walk, and a pleasant old house. You pushed your way through a revolving iron gate, and there you were in a walled garden, overlooked by the large, deep windows of the house. The walls gave shelter from the east wind that had driven into them all the way down the High Street, and for the first time that year there was sun that warmed. Even Miss Edale noticed it, and drew back her veil.

"Why, Harriet," she said, "this is really quite pleasant. If I had known it was going to be like this, I need not have worn my veil. Perhaps later in the year I can bring my lace and work at it here. It really is progressing quite fast, and do you know, Harriet, if my sum is right—I have worked it over two or three times, but then I have such a weak head for sums—I *should* be able to complete eleven yards by the end of next year. Now is that not splendid!"

But Harriet was barely listening; lace seemed such a trivial thing to get interested in. "Where shall we go now?" she asked.

Miss Edale looked worried. "Well, I do not think we will venture out of this part of the garden today; it is so sheltered. We will just stroll gently around once or twice. I do not think the conditions are clement enough yet for sitting."

Harriet looked disconsolate. This was the dullest part of the gardens, she thought. She wanted to see how the goldfish were in the lily pond, and prowl around near the glass houses, and look at the river. Miss Edale noticed Harriet's expression and, rather nervous about it, said hastily, "But if you have anything you want to see elsewhere, I would not have any objection to your going off for a few minutes or so. But do not be long, or I shall be anxious."

Harriet brightened. "I won't be long," she promised. Leaving Miss Edale to peer shortsightedly at the label on a shrub, she made her way over the neatly raked gravel to the gate in the wall that led to the goldfish pond. The fish had survived the bitter frosts of February, she was glad to see, and they flickered busily among the water plants and lilies of their pond. Harriet wondered idly whether Aunt Louisa felt sorry for them, penned up like this and having to endure ice above them, and how in any case one could know whether a fish was suffering or not.

The thought of Aunt Louisa reminded her of the bundle of leaflets under her arm which she had not yet begun to distribute. The Cornmarket and the High Street seemed to consist entirely of shops, and there had been no letter boxes in the doors that she could see. She shifted the papers rather gloomily to the other arm, and wandered off in the direction of the river. It ran around the edge of the Botanical Gardens, and went under the bridge that was crossed by the road leading out of Oxford, to lap at the foot of the walls of the college beyond. From the banks of the river in the Botanical Gardens, you could get a beautiful view of the tower of the college, rising out of the trees. Harriet, as she admired it today, realized for the first time that there was something attractive about the bare, black pencil lines of the leafless trees. She walked over the grass to the very edge of the river. It was a cold, green-brown color today, and here and there below her floated last year's fallen leaves. She looked along it toward the arches of the bridge—"so very dangerous for the young men in their punts," Miss Edale had once said to her. At that time the idea of summer and boating had seemed impossible, but now, in this early spring sunshine, she began to realize that they would one day return. It was as she raised her eyes from the arches of the bridge to the parapet above, where the road ran, that she gave a start of such horror that she nearly toppled into the river.

It was the three Smiths. There they were, leaning over the parapet in a preoccupied way. She could see the toes of six boots sticking through the stone balustrades, and above the top ledge, their three heads, black, brown, and red. They had not noticed her; they were far too intent on watching the river. Then suddenly they all disappeared. They could not have gone very far, Harriet thought; she could still hear their voices until a heavy cart, rumbling over the bridge, drowned them. Then there they were again, tilted dangerously over the ledge, and looking as though they were trying to see under the arches of the bridge.

"It was mine that won," she could hear James shouting shrilly. "Yours was miles behind, Thomas, and look, there's Joshua's there, stuck by the bridge. Joshua's *would* get stuck, just wouldn't it!"

Harriet's first thought was to rush away and hide. Then she pulled herself together, and reflected that she had a perfect right to be there, and the worst thing they could do to her was to shout rude remarks, which would not matter much, since she was all by herself with nobody to hear. She gave a hasty look around to reassure herself that this was so, and then stood her ground. But they were hammering at the parapet and arguing much too hotly to notice. Harriet felt a little disappointed. She walked nearer to see what it was down in the river that was making them argue so much.

And then, getting bolder, she thought it was a pity to waste this encounter. Why not throw a bundle of leaflets up at them, or even perhaps, very boldly, creep up into the road behind them and stuff the leaflets into their pockets? But she did not really think she had that amount of boldness, and anyway, by the time she had reached them they would probably have gone. She looked around for something heavy enough to weight the paper if she threw it, and glanced up at the parapet again to measure the distance with her eye. She gave a jump. James was staring right at her. Using a great deal of self-control not to run, she shrugged in what she hoped was a contemptuous way. But it was lost on James; almost before she had finished shrugging he had disappeared with alarming suddenness. His brothers did not seem to have noticed; they went on arguing and pointing down at the river, quite heedless of the absence of James, and the presence of Harriet below.

From the tower of the college the bells chimed the four quarters, and then a deeper bell sounded the hour. Harriet suddenly remembered poor Miss Edale, unable to move out of the shelter of the garden for fear of her neuralgia, and she moved off reluctantly, looking backward at the boys on the bridge as she went. Somewhere near the lily pond she was nearly knocked off her feet by a small boy running very fast on rather fat legs. It was James, and he was clutching a crumpled piece of paper.

Completely taken by surprise, and suddenly filled with panic, Harriet turned and fled. She ran the way she had come, hearing feet scuffling over the gravel behind her and hoarse, breathless shouting. She did not know what she was afraid of, but the more she ran the more frightened she became. She plunged in among the greenhouses near that part of the bank by the bridge where she had been standing. One of the doors was open; she flung herself in and slammed it. Crouching in a corner, in the hot, scented air, she heard James's footsteps scuttering past and disappearing into the distance. As she straightened herself up at last, she became aware of an elderly gentleman with a black umbrella, raising gray eyebrows over a pair of gold pince-nez and peering down at her with surprise. Crimson with embarrassment, she sank down again and pretended to be attending to the buttons of her shoes. After fumbling with them in a way she hoped was convincing, she stood up and marched out—straight into James, who was coming back, peering into all the greenhouses as he did so.

Once again she ran, back over that same course, around by the lily pond, breathlessly into the garden where Miss Edale was looking anxiously toward the various gates. Surely James would not attack her if she was under Miss Edale's protection? Miss Edale looked first immensely relieved to see Harriet appearing at last, and then decidedly alarmed at the way she was racing toward her.

"Harriet, my dear," she called in an agitated way. "Pray do not run like that. Whatever would your mama think!"

But Harriet did not slow down until she had reached her, and then turned around and gave James a defiant look.

"Dear me," said Miss Edale, even more alarmed at the sight of James hurling himself over the gravel with a look of ferocious determination. "This small boy—Harriet, whatever can be wrong? Harriet, there has been no accident, has there?"

"No," said Harriet, trying to control her panting, and wiping back wisps of hair from her hot forehead. "No, I don't think so. Shall we go now?" She had her back rigidly turned on James.

"But this little boy, Harriet," said Miss Edale weakly. "He seems to be in some distress. What is it, my little man?"

"Miss Edale," said Harriet, almost grinding her teeth. "*I think we had better go.*" She said these six words with great emphasis; in fact, she almost shouted them.

Miss Edale however was looking beyond her. "Dear me, I think he's going to faint. Perhaps I have my smelling bottle with me." She fumbled in her reticule in a distracted way. Harriet turned to look at James. He certainly did seem to be in a bad way. He was panting in great gusts; his face was crimson; his eyes glassy; and he was rocking from one side to another and groaning. In his hand he still held a crumpled piece of paper.

"He's not going to faint," said Harriet after staring at him for a second or so. "He's much too red. People who faint go white as chalk—I've seen them in prayers at school. He's probably got a stitch. He's been running a lot, and he's fat."

Miss Edale did not seem to have heard this remark, fortunately for her peace of mind. She triumphantly produced a tiny cut-glass bottle from her reticule. "Here are my salts, Harriet. Hold them to the little boy's nose. You had better sit down on that bench, my little man."

Harriet cruelly thrust them close under James's nose, and he gave a roar at the pungent smell, and jumped back with watering eyes. "He seems to be all right now," she said coolly. "Shall we go?"

James found his breath at last. "You can't go," he bellowed. "I want to join your side."

"Whatever does he mean?" said poor Miss Edale, dazed.

James opened the crumple of paper that he was still clutching and pointed with a rather dirty finger. "Look," he said, "that's what I want to join."

Harriet looked. It was the picture of the elephant with tears rolling down its trunk that Harriet and Agatha had pushed through the letter boxes some days ago. He seemed absolutely in earnest, and Harriet acted with great promptness. Indeed, she was rather pleased about this when she thought it over later. It was the first time she could remember that she had ever risen properly to an occasion.

"It's quite all right," she assured Miss Edale. "He only wants to subscribe to one of Aunt Louisa's charities."

Miss Edale looked a little surprised at this explanation of James's behavior. "Indeed, Harriet. Well, take the subscription from him, then. If he has quite recovered, I think we should be going now."

"Oh, but I think I ought to tell him what to do about the charity before we go. You see, he did run after me for ages."

Miss Edale spoke with determination. "He had better come along with us, then, on our way home. We really cannot wait here any longer, Harriet. We are already late, and it is beginning to turn cold again."

Harriet and James followed her out of the garden. "He can't go to America," said James shrilly, jabbing at the picture of Jumbo with his finger. "I've seen him at the Zoo—last summer—he ate buns that I gave him. They're not to let him go."

Harriet had been made far too angry by all the rude remarks she had had to suffer from the boys to accept James as an ally just like that. "Then why were you so *horrible* about it all the time?" she asked furiously.

James's voice became shriller and angrier than ever, and Miss Edale looked over her shoulder nervously. "I wasn't horrible about him. I never said anything about him at all. Fallowfield Ferox was what I said, and that's not him—that's you."

"Why did you think we wore badges with elephants on them, then, and pushed leaflets about the Jumbo Defense League through your door?" demanded Harriet, her hands quivering to shake James until his teeth rattled.

"I didn't know anything about it," said James sulkily. "I found this today in Papa's wastepaper basket, and I said what was it, and he said it was because Jumbo was going to America and good riddance. But they *can't* send him," he said, his anger breaking out afresh. "I never had a ride on him when I went, and Papa *promised* I could have a ride next time we went."

Harriet did not know what to make of it all. She thought James was the most hateful little boy she had ever met, but on the other hand he did seem to be very keen, and she could hardly let him slip through her fingers if she was in earnest about Jumbo herself.

James, however, had no intention of slipping through anybody's fingers. "Well, what are we going to do?" he demanded aggressively.

"We've got to get money to buy Jumbo food," said Harriet, trying to swallow her dislike, "and get people interested in him, and organize them to march to London and protest."

"Well, I'll do that then—march to London. It'd be jolly good—we could have swords and wave flags, and I could take my bow and arrows too, in case I saw anybody to shoot."

Harriet thought of Agatha and the flag she was embroidering, and almost groaned aloud at the sort of followers she was collecting.

"Don't be so silly," she said with fierce impatience. "Don't you understand? You can't march on London until you've got people to march, and what we've got to do is to find them."

"How do we find them? It's no good asking Thomas and Joshua. They're on Papa's side."

"We push things in through people's doors." Harriet remembered the bundle under her arm, and produced the leaflets. "Here are some, telling people that Jumbo is safe for a few days; but to make him safe for always, they've got to go on supporting him."

"Pushing things through people's doors?" said James. "I'd like doing that. Give me some."

Harriet, remembering how bad Agatha was at the same task, rather reluctantly gave him a few, thinking as she did so how very much better she could do it herself.

"This isn't many," said James critically. "We pass millions of houses on our way home. Give me some more."

The children, deep in their arguing, had been dragging far behind Miss Edale, who now stood on the curb of the road outside the Botanical Gardens, waiting for them. "Come, Harriet, you have been a very long time," she said. "We really must hasten now. Say good-bye to your little friend."

"I'm coming too," said James calmly. "Thomas and Joshua seem to have gone," he added, giving the bridge a casual glance. "I expect they're looking for me."

Miss Edale looked very taken aback, and rather alarmed. "But is there no one in charge of you?"

"No," said James cheerfully. "Aren't we going to cross the road ever?" And without further warning he darted impatiently across, right under the noses of two horses pulling a cart laden with sacks of flour. Their driver pulled them up, and their feet scrambled and slithered on the greasy surface. He leaned angrily over toward Miss Edale and Harriet. "Can't you keep a better hold on that young whippersnapper? He'd get a good leathering if he was my lad."

"He's nothing to do with us," shrieked Harriet furiously.

"Harriet, you forget yourself," said poor Miss Edale, scandalized, and looking around her in an agitated way to see who might have heard.

Over on the other side of the road James was waiting for them crossly. "What a long time you do take. You're as bad as Mama."

"You're a very naughty little boy," said Miss Edale in a shaking voice. "Now, do you know your way home?"

"Yes," said James airily. "But I'm coming back with you. I've got to help this girl push things through letter boxes. The papers she's got under her arm."

"What is this, Harriet?" said Miss Edale in a faint voice.

"It's the charity I told you about, that Aunt Louisa does." Harriet looked at James with distaste. "He wants to help."

"He can't come all the way home with us," said Miss Edale desperately.

"I'm not going to go home with you," announced James. "I want my tea."

Harriet felt relief at this, for it had crossed her mind that James might attach himself to them like a stray kitten, not to be shaken off, and follow them right to Bradmore Road and into the house. She thrust a few more leaflets at him and said, "Go on, hurry up."

James dashed off. He crossed Longwall Street, and nearly fell under the wheels of a hansom cab that was turning into it. Miss Edale gave a gasp of horror, and clutched Harriet by the arm.

"Well, anyway," said Harriet, trying to cheer her up. "He's quite far away now. Nobody will think he belongs to us."

When they caught him up he was coming out of a bookshop with a very satisfied expression on his face. "They're going to stick one up in the window," he announced. "And while I was waiting there I put them inside people's pockets and inside books. Can I have some more, please?" And again he darted off, disappearing among the passersby.

This time when they caught up with him he was hopping with great concentration on one foot, down the steps of a college. "I stuck one on the notice board," he said casually. "Did you see me do that? I hopped down all those steps, thirteen of them. I bet you couldn't do that. I think I'm going home now. I'll want some more of those things to push through people's doors. So you'd better come to the Botanical Gardens on Thursday. That's when we have our next walk."

"Harriet," said Miss Edale as James ran off. She spoke with more determination than Harriet had ever heard her use before. "We must never go to any place where we are likely to meet that little boy again. Never, do you understand?"

Chapter 9

"Jumbo Forever!"

"**H**arriet," said her mother on Thursday morning at breakfast. "That new blue dress of yours that Papa bought you seems sadly torn already. And you have hardly worn it."

Harriet looked up guiltily from her toast and marmalade. "Is it, Mama?" she said with what she hoped sounded like surprise.

"Right under the arm. You must surely have noticed it."

"Oh, yes, I do remember now. But it's only the seam, surely, Mama."

"If it was only the seam you could have mended it yourself. But the fabric has been badly ripped."

"But Mama, I wasn't careless, really I wasn't. It just tore when I lifted my arm." As she said this, Harriet remembered why she had raised her arm—it was to hurl a parcel at James. She blushed crimson at the thought of it.

"If that is really the case, then the shop must be informed." Mrs. Jessop spoke calmly, but Harriet trembled. She knew how relentless her mother could be in arguments with tradespeople.

"Perhaps it was a bit too tight, Mama," she said anxiously, and then hastily added, "But it was long enough."

"If it was too tight, then the shop had no business to let you go away in it," said her mother sharply. "I presume that you did try it on?"

Harriet nodded miserably. She saw that a battle was approaching: her mother against the shop. Her mother always won, but there would first be a good many sharp words, and rising temper, and more and more shop people called to argue, while Harriet had to sit there through it all, faint with shame.

"A year or two's time, and you will be old enough to do these things for yourself. Meanwhile, I shall have to come with you. I will never allow myself to receive inferior service from any shop, and though strictly speaking this is your father's responsibility, I must undertake it. This afternoon after school then, Harriet. Miss Edale would in any case not be coming. She wishes to go to Banbury to lay a wreath on her father's grave; it is the anniversary of his death."

"What's the matter, Hetty? You're looking very glum," said her father as he came out of his study door a little later, to find her in the passage slowly putting on her coat. "Something at school bothering you?"

"Oh, Papa," she burst out. "It's the dress. It's torn, and Mama says we've got to go to the shop and complain about it. And I do so hate it when Mama argues in shops."

Dr. Jessop shook his head approvingly. "Remarkable woman, your mother. Can't say I could ever be bothered to do anything like that myself, but she always insists on value for her money— and gets it too. She'll get another dress out of them, you mark my words."

"But Papa," wailed Harriet. "I like the blue dress. And anyway, it's all the arguing!"

Her father looked surprised. "Why, I'd have thought it was just up your street—a nice little fight like that. A girl who can

throw a parcel at a pack of boys has got no call to be frightened
of a plain argument, surely?" Then he chuckled loudly. "Don't
you worry, Hetty, you'll soon get to like it. You're just like your
mother, you know. Born fighters, both of you, never let anything go. Just like bullterriers, in fact, once you get your teeth into
anything, and it's a surgical operation to get them out."

He trod heavily upstairs, and Harriet stood still, wondering
whether she should take it as a compliment to be compared to
her mother in this way.

"What, Harriet, daydreaming again?" said her mother, appearing suddenly. "You'll be late for school. I have decided
rather differently about this afternoon. I think that it really is
time that you began to have a little independence. I disapprove
of all this coddling of young girls; it makes them quite unfit to
take their place in the world. It is, besides, rather an inconve-
nience for me to meet you at school today. So make your own
way to Thrupp and Drabble directly after school—no dillydally-
ing on the way, mind—and I will meet you there at half past
three. That will allow you a quarter of an hour to walk down,
which is ample time. It takes only eleven and a half minutes at
a brisk walk. You are not nervous about doing the walk by
yourself, are you?"

Harriet was not. But halfway through the morning, in the
middle of a French lesson, in fact, she thought of something
quite different. It was James. She was supposed to be meeting
him in the Botanical Gardens that afternoon. At least, she had
not actually said she would meet him, but he said he was going
to be there, and frightful though he was, he was a follower for
Jumbo, and she ought to forget all her own feelings in devotion
to the cause. She felt rather proud of this thought until she
remembered her father's remark that she and her mother were
just the same, like bullterriers, and she chewed her pen to
splinters, and frowned and argued with herself about whether
this was a good thing. The teacher called her sharply to atten-

tion, but while this stopped her thinking about bullterriers, she turned next to worrying about what she was to do about James. By the end of the lesson she had decided. She could not possibly get down to the Botanical Gardens and back to Thrupp's to meet her mother in the quarter of an hour that was allowed to her. So she would have to miss the last period of school. It was only a sewing lesson, and the teacher did not know the class very well, so perhaps she would not realize immediately if one of the girls was missing. Besides, people were always coming and going during that period for piano lessons, and extra drawing and dancing.

However, by the time the afternoon came, Harriet was trembling at the boldness of what she was about to do, and thinking that girls had been expelled for far less. But one ought to make sacrifices for Jumbo; she was sure Aunt Louisa would agree about that, and hadn't her mother said that she ought to start being independent? So, when the last lesson but one was finished, and the teacher had gone out of the room, leaving behind her on the blackboard a diagram of how sentences should be constructed with subjects, predicates, and objects, Harriet thrust her books and her pencils hastily into her desk, crammed the lid down on them (she heard the pencil points break as she did so), and, with her heart thumping in an agitated way, walked out. Nobody bothered to take any notice; they were fumbling in their desks for their sewing, and the class monitor was wiping the subject, the predicate, and the object off the board with great relish. Even Agatha did not look up, though she usually missed nothing; she was turned around, chattering to the girl behind her. Harriet held her head high as she crossed the hall and walked down the passage toward the cloakroom, trying not to look as though she were hurrying. But once in the cloakroom she crammed on her clothes with trembling fingers, picked up her bundle of leaflets, and ran, the buttons of her coat all done up unevenly, her hair escaping in wisps from around her hat, her gloves stuffed into her pocket.

She ran nearly all the way to the Botanical Gardens, bumping and jostling into the passersby, and feeling one moment excited by the thought of how bold she was, and the next, frightened. Supposing someone recognized her, and hastened to the headmistress to ask what one of the Oxford Ladies was doing in the town during school hours? She tried to push aside this worry, as being unworthy of her and like the way Agatha might behave, but it stuck.

The Botanical Gardens were empty, for today there was no sun, only the sharp wind which did not encourage people to linger. Harriet, breathless from walking so fast, suddenly remembered that she and James had fixed no time and no particular place to meet. She made a tour of the gardens as slowly as she could, to try to fill in the time. It seemed to last for at least an hour, but as she completed the tour and came back to where she had started, above the rumble of the cartwheels in the busy road outside, she heard the sound of the bells of the college tower chiming the four quarters of the hour. She had only been there for ten minutes, and whether James came or not, there were at least twenty more to fill up before she could take herself off to meet her mother. Meanwhile, the east wind was biting into her; her fingers felt numb through clutching the leaflets; and her cheeks raw with its keenness. She huddled her chin miserably into the collar of her coat, and stood there wondering what to do now. Then an inspiration came to her—the greenhouses! They would be warm, hot even, and she could come out occasionally to see if James was about. Then, soon after she had heard the clock strike a quarter past three, she could take herself off, her conscience satisfied that her duty to Jumbo was done.

A deliciously comforting gust of hot scented air met her as she opened the door of the first greenhouse. Safely behind the glass, it was hard to believe in the cold outside, except that she could see the wind blowing the surface of the river into little ripples. Harriet pressed her nose to the glass and tortured herself by thinking how truly horrible it would be to fall into the river today. She wandered slowly around. Luxuriant greenstuff trailed its way out of pots right up to the roof. There were not many flowers, mostly palms and ferns and tropical-looking greenery with huge shining leaves. Harriet felt desperately bored. There was not even anywhere to sit down, and she felt she ought to keep up a pretense of being interested in the plants, in case anybody came in. She walked around the cramped space about five times, dutifully peering at the labels on the plants (which were, however, all in Latin) and gazed out of the glass-paned door. She could see the bridge, and there was no sign of James on it. She decided to move on to the next greenhouse, where there might at least be a few flowers, and have a quick look around the gardens for James on the way. She did so hope, however, that he would not come.

Outside, the biting wind brought tears to her eyes, and she was thankful to retreat into another greenhouse after a few minutes. It seemed a larger one, two joined together in fact, and as she hastily banged the door shut she noticed voices in the farther one. This meant she would have to pretend harder than ever to be intent on all the plants. She walked up in the direction of the voices, and tried to peer at the speakers through the cover of an ugly shrub with leaves as huge as meat plates. But her view was blocked by something on the other side. Impatiently she began to brush the leaves aside, and then, to her horror and dismay, she found she was looking straight into another human eye. She jumped back about six feet, and a large palm standing on the staging behind her shuddered dangerously in its pot. A small figure darted around the shrub with the big leaves. It was James.

"Where've you been?" he demanded in an angry whisper. "I've been waiting here for ages."

"So have I," said Harriet furiously. "If you can't even tell me where you're going to meet me and when you're going to come, you ought to expect to be kept waiting."

"I didn't know where we'd be. It wasn't even my turn to choose a walk. It's not my turn until next week, it's Joshua's today, but he said he didn't mind changing over. He's always cold," said James contemptuously, "so he likes coming to the greenhouses. I'm never cold."

"Are the others here too?" said Harriet with horrified dismay, feeling that a mine was about to blow up under her.

"Oh, yes." James pointed through the glass that divided the two halves of the greenhouse, and Harriet now caught sight of the backs of three people bent over a plant.

"That's not your father, is it?" she asked, with even more dismay.

"Papa!" said James scornfully. "That's Mr. Ledgard—our tutor."

"Hadn't we better hurry?" Harriet felt it could only be a matter of seconds before those backs turned.

"Ssshh," said James in the most piercing tones. "It's dangerous."

Harriet was about to retort "Ssshh yourself," for James was making far more noise than she, but she stopped herself in time, thinking that it was really too undignified to quarrel with a seven-year-old. So she just shrugged her shoulders and raised her eyebrows haughtily.

"Come down here." James dragged her to the greenhouse door. "I'll keep a lookout for the others. You watch through the door. Nobody knows about me—that's what's dangerous."

"What do you mean, nobody knows?"

"They don't know about me and Jumbo. At least, I think Papa may suspect. He said something about there was a traitor in the camp. He said your aunt told him—I asked how he knew."

"That's not you," said Harriet snubbingly. "That's your maid. My aunt doesn't even know you exist."

"What, our maid Annie? Of course it isn't her who's a traitor—she only likes cats."

"Oh, never mind," said Harriet wearily. "Anyway, I should think your papa will know soon. I shouldn't think you're any good at keeping secrets."

"Of course I am," exploded James, his plump freckled cheeks going crimson with rage. "It's girls that can't keep secrets."

It was not much pleasure conducting a quarrel in hisses and whispers. Harriet would have liked to have shouted at James and then shaken him fereociously, but you could do neither when you were forever looking over your shoulder to see if there were someone coming.

"Do you want some more of these?" she said sulkily, thrusting a bundle of leaflets at him.

James pushed them inside his ulster and buttoned it up over them. "I'll have to be very careful that none of the others see," he said importantly. "I don't know what they'd do to me if they found out."

The leaflets made an extraordinary bulge inside the ulster. Harriet looked at it doubtfully. "You'd better hurry up and get rid of those, then; they make you look so queer. Anyway, how are you going to do it without anybody seeing?"

"Oh, I'll manage," said James darkly. "In fact I might do a few now. Mr. Ledgard's giving us a natural history lesson; they'll be ages yet. He thinks natural history's marvelous—I think it's stupid."

"But they'll be looking everywhere for you." Harriet was horrified at James's carefree attitude. Then she stopped. After all, why should she care? "You can do what you like, but I've got to go now." And she opened the greenhouse door.

"I'll come too," said James, and without even a glance behind him he followed her. "Mama was terribly cross with

Thomas and Joshua on Monday for losing me," he said conversationally, as they hurried up the High Street with heads bent against the wind.

"But you ran away from them!" said Harriet, outraged.

"Mama said they should have taken better care of me," said James smugly. Then, without a word of warning, he darted up to two very learned-looking clergymen walking toward them deep in conversation, and pushed a leaflet into each of their hands. Harriet wanted to collapse with horror.

"Did you see me do that?" said James triumphantly as he waited for her to catch up with him. "That's what I'm going to do. Letter boxes aren't any good. This is much better; people notice them."

And all the way up the High Street James ran breathlessly from side to side of the pavement handing out crumpled pieces of paper. Some people, talking busily, took no notice but stuffed them in their pockets without looking; young men in black gowns whistled and laughed, ladies smiled, and one elderly lady gave him a penny. Harriet walked behind, quite sick with dismay. But it was no use pretending that she and James were not together because James kept calling back to her for admiration or for more leaflets. When he was given the penny he was jubilant. "I'm going to spend it on four licorice sticks," he said, "or perhaps two licorice sticks and two sugar mice—no, a sugar mouse and a gob-stopper. I'll just go up to that sweet-shop up there, and then I'll go back to the Gardens and find the others. You'd better give me some more of those things—I might get another penny."

Harriet thrust all that she had with great violence into his hands. "You can do what you like with them," she said furiously. "I'm going now." She marched to the curb, and looked either side of her before crossing the road. Behind, a newsboy was shouting hoarsely, but she could not pick out what he said because of the rattle of the wheels passing down the street. She looked up anxiously at the clock tower at the crossroads—it said twenty-five past three, which would have been all right if her mother had been any ordinary woman. But being Mrs. Jessop, to be on time was to be late. Harriet peered doubtfully through the traffic at the shop front of Thrupp and Drabble, looking for the brisk, impatient figure of her mother. As she did so, she felt a hand clawing at her shoulder, and giving a startled jump, she found herself looking down into the angry face of James.

"They're going to send him to America, after all." He was almost choking in his rage, and tears stood in his eyes. "Look," he screamed, wrenching Harriet's arm, and pointing wildly to the placard which the newsboy had beside him. "JUMBO FOR YANKEES AFTER ALL" it said in heavy black chalk. Harriet stared at it, and tried to hear what the newsboy was shouting. But she could only pick out "Jar—mbo, Jar—mbo litest."

"Perhaps it doesn't mean he's actually going," she said at last.

"But it does mean it," howled James. "I asked that boy if he was, and he said yes."

"Give me your penny," commanded Harriet. She gave him no time, but snatched it from his hand, and went over to the boy. She and James stood at the edge of the curb, fumbling angrily with the damp sheets.

"Give it to me," shouted James. "It was my penny, wasn't it?"

Harriet gave in. Even with James tearing open the paper so clumsily, it did not take long to find the news. It was splashed all over the front page in huge black letters. "YANKS TO HAVE JUMBO. NEW COURT ORDER."

James banged one hand down on the paper. "They can't. A judge said they couldn't. What judges say is law. You ask Papa."

Harriet picked up the edge of the paper that he had let go. "Keep still and let me read it if you can't yourself."

At this moment somebody tapped her shoulder. Harriet started quite as violently as she had a few moments before with James. But this time she found herself gaping at her mother.

"Harriet, it has turned half past three," said Mrs. Jessop. "I am pressed for time; I will hear your explanations later. Is this little boy your friend?"

But James did not wait to be introduced. He wrenched at the paper; jerked it out of Harriet's hands; and she had a momentary glimpse of him pounding down the High Street, bumping and jostling the passersby, with the newspaper flapping in his hand. She followed her mother across the road in such a state of agitation and alarm, wondering just what they were going to do to Jumbo (for she had not had time to read the paper), and how she was going to explain to her mother what she was doing on the wrong side of the road quarreling with a strange boy over a newspaper, that she nearly walked into a passing cab. Her mother pulled her back and said nothing. She merely remarked as they walked into the shop: "I am afraid that I made a mistake, Harriet, and allowed you independence too soon."

The following twenty minutes were as painful as Harriet had expected, but she was already so miserable that the unpleasantness of the interview could not lower her spirits any more. First the stout lady assistant was summoned; then she was joined by the manager of the department; and finally they all went to the office of the manager of the whole shop. The stout lady said angrily that "the young lady's pa had hurried them so over it, there wasn't any time to see that the dress fitted, and anyway, he had been satisfied, hadn't he?" The manager of the department became very angry indeed and said that their goods were of very high quality and their customers must take the responsibility if they chose them too small. The manager of the whole shop pursed his lips, pulled his whiskers, drummed his fingers on the desk, and said little. Mrs. Jessop throughout was cold, calm, and reasonable, and this made everybody angrier than ever. And during it all, the wretched dress lay in front of them spread out, its rip exposed for all to see. When Mrs. Jessop reminded them that she would have to reconsider buying all the materials for the Prisoners' Self-Help from Thrupp and Drabble, they gave in, and ten minutes later she and Harriet left the shop, carrying not the pale blue dress, but a sensible brown serge one, rather too large at the moment, but it was chosen for the following winter.

Harriet trailed half a pace behind her mother, exhausted, humiliated, and as miserable as she had ever been in her life. Her throat ached with her efforts to choke back her tears, and she scuffed her boots angrily along the pavement. Everything was so dreadful—it was so cold; James was frightful; she had run away from school; Jumbo was going; they had taken Papa's dress from her. At the thought of this last misery—they had taken away her present from her—tears of self-pity welled up in her eyes, and her nose began to run. Mrs. Jessop made no remark—it was doubtful whether she even noticed.

They had just passed St. Giles Church on the weary way home when Harriet became aware of her surroundings. They had nearly reached Aunt Louisa's committee rooms. She looked around for the notice; there it was, "Jumbo Defense League." At this point her misery about Jumbo became uppermost among all the other miseries. She stopped dead. "Mama," she said thickly, "can I go in for a moment and see Aunt Louisa?"

"Harriet, we are late, and I have an appointment at five. Aunt Louisa comes to see your father on Saturday. Could you not wait until then?"

It needed only this to bring Harriet's self-pity to the surface. At that moment everybody seemed against her, and Aunt Louisa her only supporter, the only one who understood. She stamped her foot and tears, half of rage, half of misery, poured down her cheeks. "It's important, I've got to go, you don't understand. Oh, everything's so horrible today!"

Her mother looked at her with surprise. "If it is as important as that, you had certainly better go in," she said. "But I am afraid I cannot wait for you. Have you enough handkerchiefs?"

Harriet muttered something about having one, and then ungraciously turned her back and ran. She followed the direction of the rather badly drawn finger which pointed through the wide-open front door. A trail of muddy footprints led across the hall—even with her eyes half blinded with tears she could not miss that. And if she had, the sound of many angry female voices would have led her in the right direction. Forgetful of her tears, and not even knocking, she burst through the door.

There seemed to be dozens of ladies, squeezed around a rough trestle table. They were all talking at once, some of them even shouting with flushed faces and angry eyes. And there was Aunt Louisa, at the top of the table, her hat slightly askew, and more excited than Harriet had ever seen her. She saw her niece at once, scraped back her chair, stood up, and said: "There, my friends, there is the face of our English children, wet with tears. Friends, we cannot stand by and see the innocent suffer!"

There was a roar of "No," and a thunder of feet as the ladies stood up. Several of them came to Harriet and patted her and made soothing sounds. She, too astonished to cry any more, blinked at them through her tear-swollen eyes.

"Aunt Louisa, has he really got to go to America now?" she said, in her anxiety paying no attention to the other people in the room.

"Harriet," said her aunt very solemnly and impressively. "We shall fight this tooth and nail, with every quivering fiber of ourselves. We shall go to all lengths. I am ready to fling myself under Jumbo's feet, if this will help."

The ladies broke into applause at this. Some clapped, some waved, and one of them shouted, "Jumbo forever!"

Her aunt picked up some sheets of paper from the table. "Look, Harriet."

Harriet looked. She could see only names, hundreds of names, written in different handwriting.

"Our supporters," said her aunt triumphantly. "The harvest of a single afternoon alone. So, in a week, with our members working in every town, in every village up and down the land, we can gather a million names. For it is numbers alone, sheer strength of numbers, that can defeat the wicked purpose of those cowardly men."

"It's a petition to Parliament," explained one of the ladies to Harriet, nodding her head violently and smiling. "We want to get a million names on it."

"A million!" said Harriet, quite stupefied. "It's not just us, then, that belong to the Jumbo Defense League?"

There was a titter of laughter from the roomful of ladies. Miss Jessop broke in with a melodramatic voice. "Harriet, we are but as grains of sand on a shore. Our cause is nationwide. Every moment brings new hearts rallying to us." She made a sweeping gesture toward a map of England that hung on the wall. It had little flags stuck all over it. "There is a branch of our league in each of the places that is marked with a flag."

"Oh," said Harriet faintly. She was completely taken by surprise. All this time she had thought of herself and Aunt Louisa fighting a battle against the whole of England, with perhaps Agatha and James as halfhearted supporters. And now it turned out that Jumbo had millions of supporters! She did not know whether to be glad or sorry. She supposed she ought to be glad; but a lot of the excitement had gone out of the affair.

There was a rush of feet down the passage outside, and the door was flung open with such violence that it crashed back against the wall. Everybody stiffened as though this was the beginning of a siege by the anti-Jumbo party. But it was only James, hot, red, and gasping. He stood there scowling at them, holding one hand to his side, and panting for breath.

"They're going to let Jumbo go," he shouted at last, waving the newspaper that he and Harriet had bought with the penny. "They can't. They promised they wouldn't. Why doesn't somebody *do* something?"

"Another child!" said Aunt Louisa. She seemed almost frenzied with excitement. Harriet had never known her like this before; she had always seemed rather stern and cold. It seemed so odd to see her with her hat crooked, her hair escaping in untidy wisps, and one of the Jumbo badges pinned wildly to her coat. In fact, Harriet found it rather embarrassing.

Aunt Louisa walked dramatically up to James while the roomful of ladies watched, breathless. She kissed him on both cheeks and shook him by the hand. "Welcome, welcome, to our little band."

James struggled free and rubbed the back of his hand over his cheeks. "What are you going to do?" he said again with fury.

Harriet tried to put him in his place. "They're having a petition to Parliament. There are millions of people," she said crushingly.

"Well, why don't they do something, then? Kill the man who's letting Jumbo go. I'll go and kill him if you like."

The ladies tittered. Aunt Louisa crushed them with a stern frown. "This is the spirit we are trying to rouse," she cried, "and you laugh! Well said, my little man. We shall have a children's crusade and you shall lead it."

"Can we go today?" said James eagerly. "It won't take me a minute to go home and get my bow and arrows."

Harriet felt hurt. Her aunt had once promised that she could lead a crusade. "Of course you can't go today," she told James. "Don't be so silly."

"Why can't I go today? People always put things off. And if they say 'some day' it always means they aren't ever going to."

Aunt Louisa stepped forward. She took Harriet's left hand and James's right and joined them together. "There," she said, turning to her committee. "With the inspiration of these children before us, we shall march forward. And if we are ever tempted to flag, let us remember their shining examples. Jumbo forever!" she called shrilly.

And all the ladies behind her joined in: "Jumbo forever!"

Chapter 10

"When Are We Going to March?"

*H*arriet was very miserable that night. The excitement of battle had made her forget for the moment what a horrible afternoon it had been; when she heard all the ladies shouting "Jumbo forever" she had felt ready to pour out her blood for the cause. But to run home, longing for eager sympathizers to whom to tell it all, and only to find a cold house and nobody but her mother, who was quite indifferent to Jumbo—that was enough to take the heart out of anybody. Her mother had said nothing, not a word of reproach for Harriet's outburst on the way home, nothing about having kept her waiting at Thrupp's, and then having been found on quite the wrong side of the road in company with a strange boy. But this silence had perhaps made it worse, and even more humiliating for Harriet. And of course it was no use talking to her mother about Jumbo; she could expect no sympathy there. By the time she had eaten her second piece of bread and butter at teatime she could keep back her tears no longer; they trickled down her face and splashed onto her plate. She did not want to wipe them away because she was afraid that that would make her mother notice them. But in the end they came pouring down in such floods that she had to. She need not have worried; her mother gave no sign whatever of noticing that anything was wrong.

Her father was out; Harriet peeped into the study, hoping that perhaps Fairy was there. Fairy was usually a nuisance, but today it would be comforting to have her clumsy affection. Sitting in the dining room when tea had been cleared away, she found she could make nothing at all of her homework—some sums about pipes and water cisterns, and she put her head down onto the table and gave herself up to sobbing, not bothering any longer about people coming in and finding her like that.

Later, much later, her father did find her there, her face swollen, her arithmetic book smudged and blotched with tears. She had talked wildly between gulps for breath, of "Jumbo—so awful—sums" and then, "And Papa, they've taken away your dress!"

Presumably Dr. Jessop had already been told about this, for he went on busily making his calculations about the pipes and the cisterns and the amount of water, on the corner of the blotting paper, and merely said: "Never mind. Cheer up, Hetty, you've got a new one in its place, and a torn dress that's too small isn't much good to anybody."

"But Papa, you gave it to me and I loved it," she wailed miserably.

"But you couldn't have worn it much longer. You'd grown out of it almost the first time you'd put it on. That's that sum finished. Look, I tell you what, I'll buy you a really pretty hat for the spring—you won't be able to grow out of that so quickly."

The spring! Harriet could not believe that there ever would be such a thing. It had always been winter since they had been in Oxford, and it was impossible that it could ever change.

But looking out of her bedroom window the next day she

noticed, suddenly, that the buds on the pear tree in the next
garden did seem very large, and the birds were singing more
loudly than she had heard them before.

"Your aunt has sent a note asking you to go to her committee
rooms after school," said her mother at breakfast. "Frankly,
Harriet, I don't think it's a very good idea, but as you know, I
always treat you as a responsible being, and it is for you to make
the choice."

"Then I may go, Mama?" said Harriet eagerly.

"As I have said, the choice is yours. But Harriet, there are
more worthwhile things in life than elephants, you know."

Her father looked up from the *Morning Post*. "That's right,
Hetty, there are. New spring hats, for one thing, and spring
itself just around the corner. I should give Jumbo a miss if I
were you. There are enough addlepated females around him
without my Hetty joining in."

Harriet said nothing. Her parents just did not understand,
she thought. They never could, not in a million years.

Her father gave a rumble of laughter behind the newspaper.
"Why, Hetty, you've sent a telegram to Mr. Barnum. Did you
know?"

"Me, Papa?" she said, puzzled.

"You're a British child, aren't you? Well, listen to this. 'P. T.
Barnum, New York. Editor's compliments. All British children
distressed at elephant's departure. Hundreds of correspondents'—
I can assure you that I am not one of them, Hetty—'hundreds
of correspondents beg us to inquire on what terms you will
kindly return Jumbo. Answer prepaid, unlimited.' Now if I was
Mr. Barnum I'd telegraph back at once—the paper says it'll pay
for the reply—'A million dollars and I'll let him go.' And I bet
you all Lombardy Street to a China orange that your aunt and
her like would manage to whip up a million dollars in next to
no time. And just think of all the lamb chops you could get for
a million dollars. But if I wanted fifty pounds to save me from

starvation, would Aunt Louisa and the nation's children rally around me? They would not." He snorted and turned over the pages of the paper indignantly. "Every page you open has got some nonsense about this confounded elephant on it. If they don't take care I shall change to *The Times*."

"You've said that every week for twelve years, William," said his wife placidly. "Harriet, I am afraid you will be late for school unless you hurry. I shall tell Miss Edale to meet you at your aunt's committee rooms, a quarter of an hour later than usual."

Harriet walked to school feeling a great deal of dread; she wondered just who had noticed her absence the day before, and how they would deal with it. Perhaps Miss Raby herself would make a solemn announcement in prayers, and order Harriet to come forward and stand in front of the whole school while she explosed her wickedness. Or perhaps the news that Harriet was to be expelled was all over the school already, and chattering girls would seize on her immediately she arrived and tell her about it.

But the only person who took any notice at all was Agatha. As Harriet came in through the gates, Agatha stopped chattering to her particular friend Alice for long enough to say: "The flag's nearly finished. I'm going to bring it to school on Monday and show it to everybody."

"Oh, the flag," said Harriet impatiently. "Did anything happen—yesterday afternoon?"

"Happen? Why, whatever should happen? You were there yourself."

It was all very tame after all, and instead of feeling relieved, Harriet felt rather depressed. She would have liked to have made some sacrifice for Jumbo's sake. However, she was a little cheered by the thought of all the seething excitement that she would find at the committee rooms, and the important way Aunt Louisa had summoned her there to take part in it.

But at the committee rooms there was disappointment
too. There was no roomful of cheering ladies shouting Jumbo
slogans. There was only Aunt Louisa, looking very tidy and
upright and gray today, and busily addressing envelopes.

"Ah, Harriet, I am glad to see you. I have a little task for
you. Your school is a fairly large one, I think? Well, I want you
to put this notice in a prominent place there; it appeals for
child supporters for our crusade."

Harriet swallowed, and nervously clasped her hands. She did
not mind marching to London, or pushing things through
people's letter boxes, or even besieging the Zoo, but she did not
think her aunt could realize how utterly impossible it was for
her to stick up notices at the school. She, a girl in one of the
lowest classes. Why, only the head monitor would be allowed
to do that.

"Oh, but Aunt Louisa," she said weakly. "Couldn't I just ask
some of my best friends?"

"And how many friends have you, Harriet?"

Harriet considered. There was Agatha of course, and she
supposed she might say Alice and Monica; perhaps Mary and
Jessie. She firmly made it up to a round number. "Ten, Aunt
Louisa."

"And is ten enough to win a battle? No, Harriet, I think not.
A notice in every classroom, please—no, we must not stint
things. *Two* in each classroom, and perhaps the head governess
could make a point of reading it out at morning assembly."

Harriet had never been given such an impossible task in her
life, and she was wondering how she could begin to explain to
her aunt the impossibility of it.

"Come, Harriet, what is the difficulty?" said Miss Jessop
impatiently.

"But I can't do anything like that—nobody ever does. I
mean, you just *can't*," she faltered miserably.

Miss Jessop laid down her pen and stood up. Harriet watched

her with anxious eyes as she buttoned up her coat. "Are you going out?" she said timidly.

"You and I are going to your school, and I will show you personally how to set about this sort of thing—precious as my time is. It had seemed little enough to ask, but I find I was wrong."

Harriet followed her down the muddy passage to the front door, which stood permanently propped open with a heavy iron boot scraper. There, just beside the door, sheltering from the keen wind, stood Miss Edale, patiently waiting. Harriet's heart gave a thankful leap. She had completely forgotten about Miss Edale; perhaps she could rescue her from this perfectly horrible situation.

Miss Edale smiled rather nervously at Aunt Louisa. "You will forgive me for venturing to wait for Harriet just here. But the fact is I have just seen rather a tiresome little boy approaching, and I hoped I would escape his notice." She spoke as if he were a sort of savage dog. "Oh, dear me, there he is now," she said with alarm, looking at the gate.

It was, of course, James. He was grasping a newspaper again, just as he had been yesterday, and he was, as usual, panting. "Look!" he shouted to them as soon as he saw them standing there. "It's all because you wouldn't let me go and fight them." And he waved the newspaper.

Miss Jessop seemed to know at once what he was talking about, and why he was in such a state of fury. "An answer to our telegram?" she called, and ran hastily down the steps. She pulled the newspaper out of James's hand. "Let *go*, little boy," she said fiercely.

"It cost me a penny," said James truculently. "So did the one I got yesterday. That makes tuppence. I could have got eight sticks of licorice."

Harriet was more than ever disgusted with him. "Or it would have kept Jumbo alive for two minutes," she snapped at him.

Miss Jessop paid no heed to these exchanges. She was absorbed in the newspaper. "Listen to this," she said in a trembling voice. " 'My compliments to Editor *Morning Post* and British nation. Fifty million American citizens anxiously awaiting Jumbo's arrival. My forty years' invariable practice of exhibiting the best that money could procure makes Jumbo's presence here imperative. Hundred thousand pounds would be no inducement to cancel purchase. P. T. Barnum.' " She flung the paper down and trampled upon it.

"That was *my* paper," howled James, struggling to pull the bits from under her feet.

But it was doubtful whether Miss Jessop even noticed him, such was her passion. "Low, money-making brute. Sordid huckster. We appeal to his humanity, and he answers us like this!" She kicked the mangled and muddy paper contemptuously along the pavement, and James scrambled to pick it up.

Miss Edale, still standing beside Harriet on the doorstep, blinked nervously at all this violence. "But if there are fifty million people wanting to see the elephant?" she ventured. "There are surely not so many people in England?"

Miss Jessop turned to face her, and beat her clenched fists together. "And what is that to us? It is Jumbo, Jumbo's sufferings at this sordid haggling that you forget!"

"They said I could have a ride on him, and I never will now," shouted James.

"Harriet," said Miss Edale, looking at him very apprehensively. "I think we might go now."

Harriet was only too glad, and hoped that her aunt would have forgotten about the notices for the school. As they passed James, who was still scrambling to pick up the bits of his newspaper, he looked up with a flushed face and said smugly, "Thomas and Joshua have found out about me and Jumbo. They're terribly angry."

"Oh," said Harriet coldly. She was determined to be dignified and restrained this time.

"It's you they're angry with," he bellowed after her. "For
making me belong to the Jumbos."

The injustice of this, the sheer falsehood, made Harriet
seethe with rage. She could pay no attention to anything for
the rest of the day. Her father thought she was upset by Mr.
Barnum's telegram, but it was not that; it was the feeling of
how unfair everything was, and her utter helplessness to do
anything about it. She thought that all the Smiths were horrible, but she reckoned she had good reasons for thinking so, and
she did not see why they should think she was horrible for
completely false reasons. Her father, unable to rouse her with
Mr. Barnum's telegram, returned to the *Oxford Mail*. "Well, all
I can say is I hope they get this confounded elephant off to the
Yankees before he can do any more harm. I think everybody's
gone mad, and I'm sick and tired of it all. Louisa is the worst of
them all. She was bad enough about Liberty for Dogs, but this
is ten thousand times worse. I really sometimes think she is out
of her mind. Do you know, I saw her running, yes, running, up
the Banbury road this afternoon with a little boy waving a lot of
bits of paper. I think it was one of the Smith boys, now I come
to think of it. And that's a curious thing, for if ever a man is
against Louisa and her causes it's Professor Smith."

"I am sure she could not have been *running*, William," said
Mrs. Jessop smoothly. "Harriet, tomorrow is Saturday; I should
like you to come with me in the afternoon to pay some calls. I
think it will take your mind off your troubles—you seem to
have a great many these days."

Harriet hung her head. She did not know whether she
wanted to pay calls or not. But she supposed it was better than
sitting in the dining room sewing clothes for the prisoners'
babies that she never saw, and there was always the chance that
her mother might be going somewhere interesting, inside one of

the colleges, for instance, for she had never been out calling with her mother in Oxford until now, and she had no idea what sort of people she knew.

But after an hour with her mother, plodding down the Banbury road and calling on ugly great barracks of houses, she thought she did know. They were plainly dressed, sensible ladies, who sat in rather cold living rooms which were very brown and dull, and there were never any children or even animals. Instead, she would be handed an album of views of mountains and scenery to look at. After the fourth house Mrs. Jessop consulted a list.

"We have no more now until we reach the middle of the town."

Harriet, thankful to be free of the Banbury road, skipped beside her. "Oh, Mama, look," she cried. "There's a tree with flowers on it." She pointed excitedly to pale pink flowers on a leafless branch.

"Almond blossom," said her mother. "Yes, spring is late this year. Oxford is a pretty place in spring."

"Is it?" Harriet looked doubtfully at the huge red houses they were passing.

"The Banbury and Woodstock roads look different places entirely. There are a great many flowering trees in all the gardens, and all the horse chestnuts are in flower."

Harriet was amazed. She had no idea her mother ever noticed things like that. Then, as they walked down St. Giles, she looked up at the trees that lined the road. Their buds were certainly much larger than when she had last noticed them. A week or so then, and perhaps there would be spring. She gave a little skip.

They turned the corner by Balliol College, down into Broad Street. They were getting painfully near the Smiths' territory. It was just as she thought this that she saw the hateful and unmistakable James. He was lolling against a wall, sucking something. He recognized Harriet at once, and pounded up.

"Why aren't you doing something!" He stood right in front of her and looked as though he wanted to begin a fight. "I went to your school last night," he said proudly. "Your aunt took me and we stuck up notices all over the place. Just because you were too afraid to do it yourself."

"Harriet, who is this boy?" her mother asked. "He was with you the other day, was he not?"

"His name is James Smith, and he's a perfect nuisance," she said violently.

James was outraged. "Nuisance yourself," he bellowed. "If you hadn't been such a nuisance I wouldn't have had to go to your school and stick things up. Anyway, why aren't you doing something about Jumbo now?"

Harriet forgot to be restrained. "Why aren't you? You're just eating licorice."

"Harriet," said her mother, "I don't think this argument is a very profitable one. And we are in rather a hurry."

"So am I," said James, "it's nearly teatime." And he trotted along beside them. "Why aren't you doing something?" he went on complaining. "I am. I stuck those notices all over the school. Why can't we have that crusade your aunt keeps talking about?"

Harriet held her head very upright, and clenched her tongue between her teeth. She was determined not to forget herself again, and be swept into another undignified argument.

"Well, why can't we?" persisted James, running along backward in front of them. "Why?"

"Young man, you'll fall over if you don't take care," Mrs. Jessop warned him. "Does your mother know where you are?"

"I went out to spend my Saturday penny. Joshua was supposed to be coming with me, but he was reading. I couldn't help it, could I, if he was reading? So I just went."

"Joshua, James?" said Mrs. Jessop reflectively. "Can it be that you are Professor Smith's little boy? In that case we are going to see your mother; you had better come along with us."

"To see Mrs. Smith!" Harriet in her horror stood quite still. "Oh, Mama, we can't!"

Mrs. Jessop misunderstood her horror. "Of course we are, Harriet. Don't be such a silly child. Mrs. Smith will have forgotten that little episode of the parcel a long time ago."

James put in his oar. "No, I don't think she better had. Thomas and Joshua will probably murder her," he said gloatingly. "They're furious with her. Joshua isn't often furious, but he is now. It's all because of me."

"You're a very silly little boy, you know," said Mrs. Jessop calmly. "Still, I suppose one day you will grow out of it."

"Well, they are angry," said James with loud fury. "Wouldn't you be if you found a traitor in your family? And it's her that's made me a traitor." He pointed an accusing finger at Harriet.

Mrs. Jessop took no further notice of him. She tried to make things easier for Harriet by talking to her of this and that as though she were a grown-up; of the prisoners' babies, of the next Women's Rights tea party. But though Harriet was grateful, she was too wrapped up in shame and anger to listen properly.

At last they reached the Smiths' house and rang the bell. James had been talking loudly all the way down Canterbury Lane about the crusade and how he was going to march in the very front with his bow and arrows. He went back to his monotonous questioning as they stood on the doorstep. "When are we going to march, when *are* we?"

Harriet lost her temper again. "Never, I hope, if you're going to be in it."

There was no time for any more to be said, for at this moment the door was opened, and the housemaid whom Harriet had already met stood there. "Lawks, there you are, Master

James. I can tell you, the mistress is nearly off her head looking for you."

A large and agitated lady bustled up the hall toward them. "James, you naughty boy, how could you run away like that? The third time this week, too, after all Papa said to you! We have been searching everywhere for you. Five minutes more and I would have had to send for the police."

"The police!" said James with great excitement. "Oh, why didn't you? I bet you've never been looked for by the police," he said, turning to Harriet.

Harriet's mother, who never allowed herself to be excited, nor to show any trace of worry, stood calmly in the background, wearing what her daughter knew was rather a superior smile. She stepped forward now.

"Your son was not very far away. He was outside a sweetshop. I think a sweetshop is a good place to begin looking for small boys."

"Oh, Mrs. Jessop, good afternoon," said Mrs. Smith breathlessly. Then she turned to James again. "James, you're a naughty, naughty boy. You know you're not allowed to go there alone. That means there's to be no Saturday penny this week."

"I've had it," said James triumphantly. "And eaten everything."

There was the sound of heavy trampling coming down the stairs above. The schoolroom stairs, Harriet thought, with great alarm. The gas brackets in the hall trembled as somebody jumped the last few steps.

"Oh, those boys," said Mrs. Smith, forgetting James in this new worry. "I'm sure that's a new crack in the ceiling. One day soon it's going to crash down on our heads, and then where shall we be? So mind you don't do it, James." She shook a warning finger at him.

"I wasn't," said James virtuously. He calculated. "I haven't since last Wednesday, and that was only because Thomas chased me."

"And it's not only the ceiling," went on Mrs. Smith, her face creased with worry. "It's so dangerous. I met someone only the other day, Mrs. Trewbody, I think, who had a niece who broke her nose jumping down stairs."

"It's James!" shouted a voice from the top of the stairs. Harriet knew without looking that it was Thomas, and she tried to shelter behind her mother. "He's been found. Where was he?"

"Run along, Thomas dear," said Mrs. Smith distractedly. "I have visitors just now. Oh, very well then, come down just for a moment and say 'how do you do' to Mrs. Jessop and her little girl."

There was to be no escape. Harriet raised her eyes and tried to look calm. But instead of two boys, three came down the stairs. There were Joshua and Thomas, of course, but behind them a fair-haired boy with more freckles than she had ever seen on anybody.

"Here are Thomas and Joshua, my two elder boys." Mrs. Smith waved in their direction without looking at them. "And my husband's nephew, Luke Plover. Now boys, run along."

But they did not go. "Luke," said Thomas in a terribly clear voice. "This is the girl I was telling you about. She thinks animals, particularly spotty dogs and elephants, are the only things that matter. And she goes around capturing James and trying to make him think so too. I should beware of her—she's got the most frightful temper."

Everybody in the hall stood silent, staring at Thomas as he spoke, and then at Harriet. Only Joshua, still on the stairs behind him, shuffled a little uneasily, and fingered the banisters. Then, through the hush, came a thunderous knocking on the street door. With almost equal noise, a door down the hall was flung open, and Professor Smith strode out. He was in a towering rage.

"Noise, noise, noise, all afternoon. Clacking tongues, people jumping down stairs, and now this. What in the name of heaven is wrong? Is the house on fire, or is it the police?"

Poor Mrs. Smith was agitated into new alarm by these suggestions. "Oh, dear me, I do hope not. Where is Annie? She must open the door at once and find out what it is."

But before she had time to do anything about it, there was an even heavier thunder of knocking. It sounded as though somebody wanted to break down the door. Mrs. Smith, pale with fright, clung to Mrs. Jessop's arm.

Her husband marched to the street door and threw it open with such force that it hit the wall and bounced back. Outside stood Aunt Louisa. Harriet wondered why she had not realized it was her aunt there. Miss Jessop stood with folded arms and a grim expression, and looked balefully at the professor.

"Your cat," she said accusingly, "is sitting on the doorstep in this cold wind. No animal ought to be kept waiting outside in conditions like these."

Chapter 11

"Fall in, Young Ladies"

*E*very time that Harriet saw the Smiths there was some appalling scene. And after every scene she felt that nothing could now happen to make matters worse than they already were. However, it just showed how weak her imagination was, for each Smith catastrophe was worse, far worse, than the one before it. She wrote down in her score of Smith v. Jessop battles, on the Smith side, "overwhelming victory," and wondered whether it was not so overwhelming as to finish off the war altogether. The terrible things that Thomas had said about her in front of his whole family! And then for Aunt Louisa to arrive at that very moment and fan up the flames of the Smiths' anger by attacking the professor about a cat which had in the end refused to come in. What Professor Smith had said to her aunt, Harriet had luckily missed; there had been too much babble and indignation among the boys for her to hear.

She thought about it the whole of Sunday, and the more she thought the more her hatred against the Smiths grew. In fact, she lay awake for a considerable time that night trying to think of revenges she might have on the Smiths, and the tireder she became the more ferocious her thoughts grew. When Monday morning came she was listless and pale, and yawned all the way through breakfast; she tried to relieve her feelings by snapping at Fairy, who put her head blunderingly on Harriet's knee and made her spill her tea, which she did not want anyway.

Even Dr. Jessop noticed. "Let the girl stay away from school, Alice," he said. "A bit of rest never hurt anybody, especially on a Monday morning. Why should she go to work if she's got the health and strength to lie in bed?" He gave a shout of laughter and pushed back his chair from the table.

So Harriet went back to bed; her mother felt that if anybody was so unwell as not to be able to work, then they were fit only for bed. But bed during the daytime was horrible, Harriet thought as she shiveringly put on her nightgown again and crept between the cold, wrinkled sheets in the still-unmade bed. She lay there, listening to the household noises below, and feeling very cut off from the life around her. As the morning wore on she followed in her mind what they would be doing at school, with a half guilty feeling that she ought to be there with them. Though at twelve o'clock, when she knew the geography lesson would have finished, she felt a lightening of her heart—she had missed that at any rate. At one o'clock they brought her lunch on a tray, and she ate it uncomfortably in bed, wishing there was some way of balancing the tray on her knees and stopping the breadcrumbs from trickling down into the sheets. In the afternoon the housework noises stopped; a deep silence settled on the house; and Harriet slept.

She went back to school the following day feeling that months had passed to separate her from the others, and that she would never be able to catch up on all that must have happened. It was almost as though she were a new girl again. She slunk in through the gates, hoping that nobody would notice her and ask what had been wrong with her the day before. She looked furtively around the bare, trodden piece of grass that was called a garden, where the girls were clustered together talking before the bell rang for prayers. Agatha was standing with a group of her friends, chattering hard as usual. This time she was showing them something. Harriet suddenly felt lonely and more of an outsider than ever, and she went up to the huddle and peered over their shoulders. It was the Jumbo flag.

Somebody saw her at once and said her name, and instantly they all turned on her, babbling excitedly. Never in her life had Harriet had so much notice taken of her, and she stared at them, bewildered.

"You did do it, Harriet, didn't you?" urged Agatha, louder than anybody else, tugging at her sleeve. "That was why you were away yesterday? Oh, Harriet, do answer." She gave her sleeve another impatient little shake.

"Did what yesterday?" said Harriet, dazed. "I wasn't here."

"Oh, I know you weren't, but you came before school started, didn't you? To stick up those notices?"

And then Harriet wondered however she had forgotten about the terrible thing James and her aunt had done. "No, I didn't," she said violently. "I was ill. Papa told me to stay in bed. Has there been a terrible row?" she asked in a lower, frightened voice.

"Oh, yes, there was a row," said Agatha with shining eyes. "Miss Raby had the assembly bell rung yesterday in the middle of the morning. It came when we were having geography—it was so lucky. And she gave us the most awful lecture about it. So of course everybody's talking about it and wanting to join the crusade."

"Did Miss Raby want to know who had put up the notices?" said Harriet, trembling, and wondering whether Miss Raby too thought she had been responsible.

"She said she was not going to ask that. There was so much

hysteria in the town that she wasn't really surprised, but she warned us all about it. She said it was a menace to the sanity of everybody, and she hoped that the Oxford Ladies' College would set an example of good sense to the rest of the community, that we were sent to this school to be trained to be thinking women and tra-la-la-la—you know all the rest, the usual stuff."

"But . . . but you've got the flag there," said Harriet in a great state.

"Of course I have. After what Miss Raby said I sat up till long past bedtime, *and* got the maids to wake me up at half past six. We've got to inspire people, don't you see?"

Harriet forgot all her doubts, all her horror at what her aunt had done, and felt a surge of excitement. She was no longer alone. She had got the whole school behind her. It was a most inspiring feeling. And if the bored and apathetic Agatha could be roused like this, there was great hope. But the bell for morning prayers went just then, and there was no time for more explanations.

"Mary and Clementine say they're going to give their names to your aunt to go on the crusade," Agatha told her breathlessly as they ran to the cloakrooms. "And Geraldine and Beatrice are going to give subscriptions. Isn't it marvelous!"

Harriet could feel the excitement. As they stood lined up in the corridor, waiting to march into prayers, although there was supposed to be silence there was positively a hum of whispering, which the monitors did nothing to stop. Nobody lolled today. They stood tense and gestured and signaled to each other. And when they marched into the assembly hall and saw that the second mistress was occupying Miss Raby's position on the dais there was an audible murmur. Miss Raby had the health of a Samson, and, like Mrs. Jessop, disbelieved in illness, but on the very rare occasions that she was absent in London, conferring with the great Miss Buss of the North London Collegiate

School, the Oxford Ladies felt a great lightening of the atmosphere. Free from the scrutiny of her steely eye, they relaxed.

In the classroom the feeling of freedom showed itself with more signaling, and messages were mouthed by one girl to another whenever the mistress turned to write something on the blackboard. Notes were passed from desk to desk, and Agatha even managed to throw one from the front row to the back. The girl at the desk next to Harriet started tapping softly on her desk with her ruler, and smiling around the class. Within one minute everybody else had picked up rulers, pencils, pens, and were tapping out the same thing. The room sounded like a carpenter's shop. Miss Wheeler, who was deep in a diagram of a geometry problem on the blackboard, did not notice at first. It was only when somebody began to sing the words of the tune they were tapping: "Alive said to Jumbo," accompanying herself with a ruler and a pen, that she turned around. But before she could expostulate, Agatha, with flushed cheeks and almost a feverish look in her eyes, stood up and said "Jumbo for England!"

And the rest of the class, as excited as she, shouted what seemed to be the rest of the slogan: "Preserve our noble elephant. Amen."

After this remarkable outburst, there was, of course, a great deal of anger on Miss Wheeler's part, and the next five minutes were spent in dealing out punishments to the whole class. Harriet, for the good of the cause, accepted her punishment meekly, although she had done nothing this time to deserve it. Then she looked down at her desk and saw somebody else's blotting paper, a huge sheet of it, lying there. Her neighbor gave her a ferocious jab in the ribs, and whispered, "Open it."

Very gingerly Harriet did so when Miss Wheeler had returned to the blackboard. She dropped it as if she had been burned when she saw inside a picture of an elephant, and the title above it: "Jumbo's March."

When Miss Wheeler had disappeared through the door at the end of the lesson, Agatha sprang at her. "You didn't look properly," she said angrily.

"How could I?" Harriet said weakly.

"You easily could have. Look now." And she flipped over the pages. "I'm learning to play it," she said importantly. "I must have it right by Friday because I want to burst out with it at my music lesson. Won't Miss Richardson have a shock when she's expecting to hear that horrible, dull old Czerny. You can put real expression into this. Look." She pointed to the first section, headed "Jumbo's March Around the Zoo." "You play that *grandioso*—very grandly, you know. And there's 'Jumbo Being Fed by his Juvenile Friends,' 'Children Mounting on Jumbo,' 'Jumbo's Wrath on Hearing that Barnum Has Bought Him' —that's rather difficult—'Coaxing Him to Start on His Journey,' 'Alice's Despair!' " she babbled on, turning the pages. "The bit about Alice is terribly good. It makes me cry when I play it with expression. It's fairly easy too. I might miss out the bit about his wrath and play this twice over instead."

At this point she was cut off by the teacher who was coming in to take the ancient history lesson, and as she had an eye almost as steely as Miss Raby's own, in this period at least the class behaved in a seemly way, though Harriet fully expected an outburst when Hannibal's elephants were mentioned.

"We're going to have a Jumbo parade in the playground at break," Agatha said importantly when the lesson was over, "to practice for when we march to London. Miss Jessop said she was going to hire a sergeant to drill us because she does want the Oxford people to march smartly. And do you know, we're going to carry my banner!"

They practiced on the part of the playground which belonged by tradition to the Middle and Junior schools. Agatha went in front holding the banner, and tried to control everybody else as they marched in lines of four behind her. It was rather difficult, for she had to keep her head turned over her shoulder, and this made her trip over the pole of the banner, and over the roots of the horse chestnut trees that edged this part of the playground. Harriet slouched along in the back row, aggrieved that Agatha seemed to have taken over command, but a little glad that she was finding it so difficult. The girls in between them were fairly enthusiastic, but not very good marchers. They were continually out of step, and some of them nibbled apples and chattered as they went around and around the playground. A few of the senior girls watched, mildly amused.

"Oh, it's too bad," said Agatha, once again nearly falling headlong over the pole of the banner, while the front row of the marchers giggled. "Stop laughing. Monica, put down that apple. You can't get any more off it—you know you can't."

"Yes, I can," said Monica. "I can eat everything on an apple except the stalk, though you've got to take care that bits from the core don't get stuck between your teeth."

The rest of the ranks tittered, and Harriet, in the back row, thought how awful girls were. Agatha tripped over her pole again and flung down the banner.

"You're just not trying, any of you. You wait till the sergeant comes, that's all."

"When is the sergeant coming?" Harriet asked as they took off their coats a few minutes later.

"Oh, I don't know," said Agatha, who was in a very bad temper. "Your aunt just said she was getting one, but I should think it would need about twenty sergeants to get those idiots of girls to do anything." And she was sulky for the rest of the day, though in the excitement nobody noticed it. It was not only Jumbo that was causing the excitement, though that was the main cause. It was also the fact of Miss Raby being away. Somebody had it positively from the second mistress herself that she had not gone to see Miss Buss, and wild rumors flew around about what might have happened to her. Somebody said that she had gone to present a petition about Jumbo to the Queen; somebody else that she was getting married; but everybody agreed that the school was a different place without her, and babbled without stopping at luncheon, in between classes, and even during them.

But even so, they could not shake off the feeling of Miss Raby's ever-watchful eye in just a day, and the Oxford Ladies thronging down the corridors after school was over, were almost turned to stone at the sight of Agatha running, actually running, toward them. "He's here now!" she said. "At least I think it's him. The sergeant who's going to drill us."

At this everybody ran, and the fortunate few in front got a glimpse, as they peered around the door, of what was undoubtedly a soldier, standing right in the middle of the playground, with Miss Jessop beside him. He was rather a small man, with waxed mustaches so long and straight that it looked as though he could almost use them to run his enemies through and through. His uniform was so spotless and creaseless, his belt so white, that it was difficult to see how he could move without damaging it. The Oxford Ladies pushed and jostled around the door, and looked at him with the greatest curiosity. Miss Jessop said a word to him, and he marched forward.

"Now then, now then, now then," he said in a hoarse, rasping voice. "Fall in, please." Then, as there was some delay and uncertain murmuring among the girls, he said with a throaty snarl that made them all jump: "Fall in, I said."

"Fall in, young ladies," said Miss Jessop, clapping her hands. Her voice sounded thin and light after the sergeant's.

But there was no need for her to say anything. The startled girls had huddled into the center of the playground and were anxiously trying to make a line.

"Put down all that luggage you're carrying. Where do you think you're off to," he bawled at a fat little girl who had a small case in her hand, "the Con-tin-ong? Well, you're not,

see. You're here for twenty minutes with me to try to put a bit
of discipline into you. See? Now drop all that nonsense you're
carrying. I said drop it. And that means every man jack of
you," he roared at Harriet, who still had a book under her arm.

The girls formed themselves into a long, bulging line, divid-
ing their attention between trying to straighten it, and trying
not to annoy the ferocious little man any more. But their efforts
were not very successful. He flew at them like an angry terrier
dog, and began prodding at the toes of their boots with the
stick he carried under his arm.

"In with you," he barked at the startled Agatha, who was a
few inches too far forward. "Who do you think you are? The
Queen of Timbuktu? Well, none of you are no better than the
rest on this parade ground, so none of you push yourself forward, see."

With the same furious energy he marched down the back of
the line, roaring that they looked like a box of kippers that had
been open too long, the way they were standing, and poking
his stick into the backs of the worst of them. He made them
right dress, and the fat little girl came in for a lot of sarcasm
because she looked over her left shoulder. Harriet, screwing
her chin rigidly over her right shoulder, suddenly caught sight
of Miss Edale, standing outside the palings with her eyes fixed
anxiously on her. And as Harriet looked, Miss Edale waved and
then beckoned. But there could not be any escape from the
parade ground for the next twenty minutes. The sergeant formed
them up in fours, which took a great deal of work, and then
finally bellowed at them to forward march. There was no nib-
bling at apples this time. The girls marched, trying to hold
their backs like pokers, and keeping their eyes fixed nervously
on the sergeant, who stood in the middle of the playground
waving his stick.

"Left—left—left," he called out in time to his stick. "Now
then, now then, take your eyes off me, I'm not your sweetheart—

nor that blooming elephant of yours neither. You keep your eyes straight ahead; I'll let you know before you run up against the trees. Though if I tell you to march into the trees you'll march into them. Straight to the blooming top, d'ye hear. Now then, left—left—left—left."

Swinging her arms vigorously, and striding out in the back row, Harriet realized she was enjoying it. It was great fun to be doing the thing properly, rather inspiring, she thought, and as they went around and around the playground she imagined herself marching to London to rescue Jumbo. How splendid it would be if there was music. As they wheeled around the top of the playground for the fourth time or so, with Harriet at the outside edge, taking enormous strides to cover the extra distance, she noticed Miss Edale peering anxiously through the railings and trying to convey some urgent message to her. But she was under military orders and could not respond. With her eyes fixed remorselessly ahead she marched past.

The sergeant kept them for ten more minutes, tried to get them to halt in good order, shouted, stamped, and told them they were enough to make the cherubim weep. Then he finally halted and dismissed the whole parade. As they fell out he took off his pillbox hat, wiped his face in an enormous red and white spotted handkerchief, and, speaking in quite a mild voice, said: "Your pardon, young ladies. Didn't mean to hurt any of your feelings, I'm sure, but this lady"—he nodded toward Miss Jessop— "asked me special to forget you was the fair sex and treat you like my own lads at Cowley. No offense though, I'm sure." He put back his hat, drew himself up with a smart salute, and marched off.

The girls watched him admiringly, and Harriet, collecting the book she had dropped at his orders, thought rather wistfully how fine it must be to be a soldier, and wished she could go to Cowley Barracks to see them drilling there. So she felt rather peevish when she was pounced upon by Miss Edale just outside the school gate; she had in fact completely forgotten about her.

"Harriet, you are sadly late," Miss Edale said breathlessly. "I thought you would never come. What have you been doing, marching around like that?"

"We were being drilled," said Harriet loftily, "by a sergeant major from Cowley Barracks."

"It seems a very curious thing for young ladies to be doing. I wonder at Miss Raby allowing it. And now I fear we shall be too late," she said in a voice trembling with despair.

"Too late?" echoed Harriet. "But what for?"

"My lace, Harriet. Such an opportunity—something I had never dared hope for—but it's too late now."

Chapter 12

Peace Negotiations?

When Miss Edale told the story of the lace, even Harriet, wrapped up as she was for the moment in the Jumbo crusade, felt rather sorry and ashamed. It seemed that the vicar of the church in Banbury where Miss Edale's father had himself been vicar had come to hear of the lace. Would Miss Edale consider making a piece like it, he had written to the vicar of the church in Oxford that Miss Edale attended, for an altar cloth for his church? He was in Oxford at the moment, and could talk matters over with her, if they could, in spite of the short notice, meet that afternoon. And now it was too late. The time of the appointment had passed, and the opportunity was lost forever.

Harriet, as she walked beside Miss Edale on the way back to Bradmore Road, tried to tell her that the situation was not as hopeless as all that. It was only half an hour late now. They could still go to the vicarage in St. Cross Road and the Banbury clergyman might still be there. Miss Edale shook her head; her duty to Mrs. Jessop demanded that Harriet should now be returned to Bradmore Road to tea. Or Miss Edale could go alone, Harriet persisted; she herself could perfectly well find her own way home. To all this Miss Edale shook her head, with an expression of deep dejection on her face. It was no use. She must just give up thinking about it, but it would have been such a wonderful thing, and how pleased her dear father would have been. . . . Harriet could not understand such an attitude of despair when there seemed so many ways of putting it right.

"Why can't you go and see the Oxford vicar?" Harriet went on. "He would tell you about the other vicar, his name and things, and then you could write. Oh, Miss Edale, please do. Let's go tomorrow afternoon, both of us. I'll be really quick out of school."

And Harriet went on persisting like this for so long that poor Miss Edale eventually gave way, more because she always found it so difficult to argue with Harriet than because she really wanted to.

Miss Raby was still absent from school the next day, and the news went flying around that she had sprained an ankle and was likely to be away for at least a week. A wave of exhilaration spread through the lower half of the school.

"It's really what I've prayed for," Agatha confided to Harriet. "I mean," she added hastily, "nothing too bad, but just something so that she couldn't come to school for a little while. And a sprained ankle's rather nice; you just sit with it on a cushion and eat sweets and read. Do you know, even Beatrice admits that it's rather nice without her, and for someone like Beatrice to say so!" Beatrice was eighteen, and a monitor.

Harriet privately agreed with Agatha about how much nicer it was without Miss Raby. She always used to examine the dais hopefully day after day as they filed in for prayers, hoping that perhaps she would not be there (nobody surely could be well every single day of her life), and thinking rather guiltily how

pleasant it would be if something quite painless had happened
to her, like losing her memory.

To celebrate Miss Raby's second day of absence, the entire
school were wearing Jumbo Defense League badges, which Miss
Jessop had, according to Agatha, handed out at the end of
yesterday's parade, though Harriet, in her anxiety about Miss
Edale, had missed this. It was an open defiance of the school
rule that no jewelry should be worn, but even the monitors
were wearing them.

"Beatrice said you couldn't call it jewelry," said Agatha. "I
asked her last night. She said jewelry was an ornament, and
this isn't any ornament." She peered down at the ugly printed
disc festooned with ribbon which had replaced Aunt Louisa's
first badges.

If the second mistress noticed the scores of badges at prayers
she made no remark. She was a large jolly woman, with rather
untidy hair, and had a fondness for animals, especially cats.
The girls skipped in the corridors on their way to the classrooms, and one or two very bold ones even sang.

"You went away very quickly yesterday, Harriet," said Agatha
accusingly. "You missed all the badges and your aunt's speech.
Are you going to stay longer this afternoon?"

"I can't stay at all today," said Harriet guiltily. "I told Miss
Edale I'd go with her to do something."

Agatha raised her eyebrows and looked her up and down.
"Goodness me, and who was telling me last week that I was a
traitor?"

But Harriet had to endure worse things from her aunt when
she went out after the end of school. She was standing with the
sergeant near Miss Edale at the school gates. At first she smiled
at her approvingly.

"This shows praiseworthy eagerness, Harriet," she said.

"Well, actually, Aunt Louisa," said Harriet uncomfortably, "I
can't stay tonight. I've promised to do something else." She

searched for something to placate her aunt. "Everybody seems very excited about Jumbo. They're all wearing the badges, even the monitors. I should think you will get a lot of people to join the crusade."

"I hope to have the allegiance of the entire school," said her aunt calmly, "with the exception perhaps of yourself, whose support we seem to have lost." She surveyed Harriet's coat, which had no badge on it.

Harriet looked down guiltily. "I'm afraid I wasn't here last night when the badges were given out, but perhaps I could have one now."

"No matter, Harriet, no matter. Faint hearts are of no use to our cause. That is the fine thing about persecution of noble causes: It fans the flame into new life, and exposes the faint hearts who are of no use to us. Your headmistress persecuted our cause, and see what flames it has fanned." She gestured toward the school where the girls were now pouring out. "And look at the faint heart it has shown up."

Harriet, crimson with mortification, looked timidly at the sergeant, wondering if he had heard all this. But he was looking straight in front of him, with a face as expressionless as a post. She pulled Miss Edale's hand, and together they hurried off, Miss Edale with clear relief, Harriet with shame and despair. Harriet trotted along beside her, not trusting herself to speak. Being humilitated by the Smiths was bad enough, but they were, after all, enemies. But to be publicly disowned by someone she thought was her ally!

Miss Edale, sensing that something was wrong, tried to please Harriet by choosing a route that she thought she would like, in spite of her own worries about what she was going to say to the vicar, and whether he would not think she was very forward. But Harriet was too miserable to notice where they were going, or to enjoy the soft, warm spring air.

"See, Harriet," said Miss Edale as they came out of the

darkness of Holywell Street, where the houses seemed almost to touch each other across the road, into the light and space of Longwall Street. "The trees are nearly in leaf. It will not be long now before spring is with us." And she pointed to the trees that appeared over the immensely high wall that ran the length of the street. Certainly the buds had swollen and burst out and the shape of leaves could be seen, but Harriet was hardly in a mood to care. Miss Edale stopped and looked anxious.

"Mr. Furnival's house is just down there." She pointed to a house in a road that turned off Longwall Street. "You really think I ought to call, Harriet?"

Harriet knew she had to speak firmly. "Yes, I really do, Miss Edale. After all, that vicar from Banbury may be waiting to know about your lace, and if he doesn't know your address he can't write, can he?"

"Very well, then," said Miss Edale reluctantly. "If you are sure it is my duty."

They walked a little way down the road, and rang the bell of a large redbrick house that had its windows hidden with heavy lace curtains. It was just like the houses that Harriet had visited with her mother on Saturday, and she knew exactly what would happen inside; she would have to sit on a tall chair with a shiny leather seat, her feet just not able to reach the ground, and look at a heavy album of pictures of mountains while the grown-ups talked on and on and on. She felt she just could not bear it; she was miserable enough already, and the day was so warm and springlike. An elderly maid with rather a stern face opened the door, and Miss Edale, her voice trembling a little, asked to see Mr. Furnival.

"I think I'll just go for a little walk in the Botanical Gardens, Miss Edale," said Harriet boldly. "I'll come back and meet you here when the clock strikes a quarter to four."

Miss Edale's face took on an expression of alarm, horror, and consternation at this very odd proposal of Harriet's, and she hesitated at the threshold of the door in an agony of doubt, while the maid watched with grim impatience.

"Good-bye, Miss Edale," Harriet said politely, and walked away. And Miss Edale called helplessly after her, "Harriet, my dear, do pray be careful when you cross the road, and mind you come back in a few minutes, Harriet," before the door was closed behind her.

Harriet walked back toward Longwall Street rather happily. She had a quarter of an hour to wander around by herself and explore, and the leaves were nearly out and the sun was hot on her cheek. She skipped for pleasure, and then began to do something that was never possible in the company of grown-ups, trying to avoid the lines on the paving stones, which meant sometimes shuffling with tiny steps, and then taking giant strides. She was brought up sharply by the sight of somebody's boots ahead of her. She looked up; it was Joshua Smith. He stood there, staring at her silently and with what seemed to Harriet to be implacable hatred. She threw away all courage and dignity, brushed past him, and ran blindly down Longwall Street. But out of a gateway in the wall another figure appeared: Thomas Smith.

"Fallowfield Ferox," he said jeeringly, "and running too. What's frightened you? Spotty dogs or cats or elephants, or what?"

There was a scuffle of gravel, and James pushed his way through. "She's a coward," he shrilled. "She was afraid to stick up notices in her own school. I had to do it for her."

It was like a hideous nightmare, Smiths wherever she looked, all hating her. She looked around wildly; Joshua was coming up behind her. So she ran on and on, down Longwall Street, and behind her she thought she heard shouts and pursuing footsteps. She burst into the sunlit High Street and ran on down it toward the college that was lapped by the river, with some idea of crossing there and bolting into the Botanical Gardens, where it would surely be easier to hide yourself than in a bare street. Panting, and with a terrible stitch she hesitated on the curb opposite the gardens, but the street was full of traffic, slow-moving wagons and carts, cabs whisking past; she could never thread her way through that; she was trapped. She looked behind her. Under a low archway there was a door that must lead into the college, and inside, in a grassy courtyard she could see people moving about. She wheeled around and plunged through, right into the very precincts of the college.

Once inside, she was terrified at what she had done. There was a dark little tunnel where crowds of young men seemed to be lounging; she must get away from that before any of them noticed her and ordered her away. And hurrying, she emerged into the grassy courtyard. But it was no good lingering there; it was far too exposed, and she dived under another archway on her right, and found herself in some cloisters. She had never seen such things before, only in pictures, and agitated and panting as she was, she still had time to think that it was the most beautiful thing she had ever known. She propped herself against a wall and looked. The arches in front of her threw great patches of sunshine on to the stone pavements, and through them she could see a square of lawn like green velvet, and beyond it, the cloisters on the other side. Feeling bolder, she walked across the paving stones, and, leaning on a parapet that was warm with sun, she looked out through an arch. There were curiously carved figures of beasts adorning the roof of the cloisters, and she peered out and up at them. Above, the pale blue sky had small patches of hurrying white cloud. She forgot about the Smiths who were chasing her, and sighed with pleasure, and leaned out farther. From the next archway another head peered out. They looked at each other; it was the Smiths' cousin.

Startled and horrified, she scrambled back. So did the Smiths' cousin, and two children stood in the cloisters eyeing each other, Harriet defiant and ready to turn and flee.

"I know who you are," said the boy. "You're the girl who came to my uncle and aunt's house last week. I remember this on your coat." He pointed to the rows of sky-blue braid on the navy-blue serge.

"What a funny thing to remember," said Harriet, surprised out of her alarm and suspicion. "I don't think it's very unordinary. I should think a lot of girls at school must have coats like it."

"Well, there aren't many girls in our village at home," he said in a matter-of-fact way. "And this is only the second time I've been in Oxford."

He seemed quite friendly; Harriet was amazed that any relation of the Smiths could behave like an ordinary human being, and not like a man-eating tiger. "Are your cousins with you?" she asked, looking around nervously, expecting the whole tribe to be lurking somewhere behind the columns of the cloisters.

"They went off somewhere, to look at the gardens or something."

"Do you like them?" she asked, feeling very bold.

"Well, I like them better when they're staying with us at the rectory; we do things together then. But here they've got their lessons, and when they aren't doing them they're reading or playing chess or playing with James's soldiers, or something."

She was astounded to hear that the Smiths had such mild ways of amusing themselves. She had always thought of them, lately, as spending their time roaring around looking for new victims to attack. "Do you like your uncle?" she asked, more boldly still.

The boy became more enthusiastic. "Oh, yes, *he's* good fun."

"Good fun?" said Harriet in astonishment. "Professor Smith?"

He looked rather indignant at the violent way she said this. "Yes, of course he is, and very kind too. You don't know him, do you?"

She was rather abashed. After all, the professor was a relation of this boy's; she really should not have gone so far. "I
have seen him quite a lot of times," she said apologetically,
"and every time he's been furiously angry."

"Uncle Alfred? Well, I've never seen him angry, anyway. He
roars a bit now and then, but it's only pretend, really."

"What about last week, then?" Harriet demanded. "Was that
pretend?"

"Oh, about that cat. Well, I do think it was silly knocking so
loudly just about a cat."

Harriet could not deny this, but she was not going to give in.
"He roared even louder."

"You're roaring pretty loudly yourself," said the boy coolly.
"They'll hear you."

"Who will?"

"The people you're hiding from."

"It's your cousins, if you want to know," said Harriet defiantly.

"What, Thomas and Joshua and James?"

She nodded, with her lips trembling, and realized that, once
again, she was nearly crying with rage. "They attack me every
time they see me."

"Attack you? What do they do, then?"

"Oh, just shout things, awful things, in front of everybody.
You saw, didn't you? They try to make out that I don't think
about anything except elephants and spotted dogs. And now
they say that I've made that awful James the same. As if
anybody could *make* him do anything!" she finished up furiously.

The boy looked as though a problem had been solved for
him. "Oh, now I know who you are—you're Fallowfield Ferox
that they're always talking about."

"What do they say about me?" demanded Harriet furiously. "I
bet it's all untrue."

"Oh, they say you and all your family are carrying on a sort
of war against them and Aunt Edith and Uncle Alfred."

Harriet was stunned and speechless by the brazen untrueness of this version of the feud. Her voice, when she was able to speak, was shrill with indignation. "But it's *them*. What have *we* done?"

The boy did not seem particularly interested. "Oh, I don't know. They told me things, but I've forgotten. Something about liking animals better than people and setting dogs loose in Aunt Edith's bedroom and stealing away James. Uncle Alfred's quite sure that your aunt is trying to make him go mad. He says she just waits until he's settled down in his study and then she comes and knocks at the door and talks about cats or elephants, or something. He can never bear being disturbed when he's working anyway, but when it's about cats or elephants . . . !"

Harriet was in despair at this account of things. "But it's all wrong," she said at last. "All wrong. Papa didn't let the dog into Mrs. Smith's bedroom—it just followed him. He let it in because he thought it was their dog. And I never stole James—he just came. I don't know what to do with him. Can't you *tell* them?"

The boy was balancing on his heels and swinging himself around first to the left, then to the right. "It's that that's making Joshua so angry, about you taking away James, and turning dogs loose on Aunt Edith. He's never cross about anything usually. I'll tell him that you didn't, then. Have you seen the fishes in the river?"

Harriet said that she had not. He led the way around the cloisters, under another archway, and into a garden that seemed full of the warm smell of spring flowers. A stone bridge led from it, over a shallow river. The boy hauled himself up on the parapet on his elbows, and peered down into the water. "Look, there are shoals of them."

Harriet leaned over beside him. At first she could see nothing, but then she made out black shadows, flickering rapidly through the weeds on the stream bed.

"I wonder what they are," said the boy. "I've never seen ones like them before."

But Harriet did not bother to wonder. The movement of the water flowing below them, the warmth of the stone against her were so pleasant and so soothing that she felt she could stay there for hours and hours without noticing the time. The boy turned and looked at her curiously.

"Are you one of the people who want to stop this elephant from going to America?"

Harriet suddenly felt less sure about Jumbo than she ever had before. But she tried to behave as though she cared deeply. "We're marching to London to save him," she said impressively.

He gave a guffaw of laughter. "You're going to march to London to save an elephant? Well, I think you're mad!"

"Why?" said Harriet defiantly.

"Well, an elephant! And it'd take you days to walk to London—I once walked ten miles and it took me three hours and I was pretty tired after that, I can tell you. London's miles more than ten miles. And anyway, what would you do when you got there? Is it just going to be girls? I don't suppose they'd allow you near the elephant."

"There'd be boys too," said Harriet feebly. "From all over England. It isn't just girls."

"Boys like James. Just think, an army of boys like James." In spite of herself, Harriet laughed. "Well," the boy went on; "I think people who get worked up like that about an elephant going to America must be as mad as the people Uncle Alfred talks about, who will take away a cabman's horse and send it for a holiday and not care if the cabman starves to death."

And Harriet realized that this was just what Aunt Louisa would do, and she was silent. The chimes of the clock came through the warm afternoon.

"Quarter to four," said Harriet, startled. "I've got to go."

"I suppose I'd better try to find Thomas and Joshua. They're probably looking for James."

"You can tell them I haven't stolen him, anyway."

They laughed as they hurried back the way they had come, first the garden and then the cloisters. Luke tilted his head back, and looked up at the carvings high in the vaulted roof.

"I'd like to paint them," he said, "red and gold and blue, I think." As he said that he blundered straight into a tall, very senior-looking man in a black, flapping gown who came striding past.

"Oh, no you don't, my little man," he said, wagging a finger, not in Magdalen College—let lesser colleges do what they like, and don't you go picnicking on our grass either."

"We wouldn't dream of it, sir," said the Smiths' cousin, offended.

"Whether you would dream of it or not is beside the point," said the man in a thoroughly friendly voice. "But let me tell you, young man, that only yesterday I came across an entire French family lunching on our grass. They were actually slicing their sausage when I saw them. My friends, I said, now would you partake of luncheon in the middle of the Louvre Museum? Would you, I asked? And do you know, they said they would." The man gave a bray of laughter, and walked on.

The children watched him disappear, his hands clasped behind his back under his gown, so that it looked like the tail of some grotesque blackbird.

"I think he must be rather mad," said the boy.

"Papa says that they all are a bit mad, the people who have anything to do with the University," said Harriet. But all the same, she felt it was delightful having been talked to as an equal by a senior person in the University. Then she stopped suddenly outside a door that seemed to lead to a chapel. "Oh, listen," she said. She had never heard singing like it—boys'

voices like threads of silver, men's voices deep below them, a
wonderful pattern of sound that echoed around the sunny
cloisters.

"It's Magdalen choir," said the boy. "It's famous."

"I didn't know there could be singing like that," said Harriet
reverently. As she stepped out from the college gateway into
the High Street she felt that just in this one afternoon she had
discovered more about Oxford than she had in the whole of the
five months she had been there. The boy had gone off to some
other part of the Magdalen gardens to look for his cousins, and
as Harriet walked toward Longwall Street she thought she did
not care what happened, even if three ravening Smiths burst
out at her.

But they did not. Longwall Street was sunny and deserted,
and in St. Cross Road not even an agitated Miss Edale was to
be seen seeking her charge. Harriet leaned against the railings
of the vicarage and waited. She was not kept long. Miss Edale's
voice was heard rather tremulously saying good-bye to someone
within the door, and then she came hurriedly down the steps.

"Oh, Harriet, how thankful I am you are here. I cannot
think what possessed you . . . But never mind that now. What
do you think has happened? Such distinction as I have never
dreamed of! My lace, when it is complete, is to be part of an
altar cloth for the cathedral. The cathedral, Harriet! Oh, but I
shall have to write to the vicar at Banbury to offer him a piece
like it since he was the first to ask for it. If only my dear father
had lived long enough to hear of this, how proud he would be!"

It seemed that when Miss Edale had called on Mr. Furnival,
she had found him talking to a dignitary from the cathedral.
Miss Edale had been far too overwrought to discover just who it
was. He had inspected the lace with great interest, had said
that he did not know that it was made in England, and had
begged her, if ever she made any more, to allow the cathedral
to use it. "And of course I said, Harriet, that if he thought this

piece was worthy enough he could have it as soon as it was complete."

"But if I hadn't said you ought to go and call on Mr. Furnival, then the cathedral clergyman wouldn't ever have seen your lace?" said Harriet, slowly working it out.

"That is so, Harriet. I owe it all to you. Oh, I can't tell you how happy I am."

And Harriet felt almost as elated and pleased herself. So much so that when there was a scuffle of feet behind her which she instantly recognized as James's, she turned around quite calmly and waited for him.

"I think the others are looking for you," she said to him severely.

He took no notice of this. "When are we going on this crusade?" he demanded. "I'm all ready. If we don't hurry, there won't be anybody to fight. Oh, tell them to hurry."

"Go and tell my aunt yourself, then. You'd better go—I can see your brothers running after you."

"I don't want to tell people. I want to do something," said James furiously.

"You'd better come along and do some drill with the girls at the Oxford Ladies' College, then. They're practicing to march to London." Having delivered what she hoped was a crushing snub, Harriet turned as haughtily as she could, and marched off.

"When shall I come?" James shouted after her.

"Oh, any afternoon after school—and be sure to ask for Miss Raby first."

Chapter 13

James on Parade

*I*n spite of all the humiliations of the earlier part of the afternoon, she had enjoyed herself. "Oxford's so beautiful," she kept saying excitedly to her parents. "And Papa, the singing!"

"And you have only just discovered that Oxford is beautiful?" said her father, teasingly.

"Well, you see, it was so cold before and everything. I just didn't seem to bother to look."

"Poor old Oxford, it's been here nine hundred years, ten hundred years, and you've only just noticed it. Well, Hetty, nine hundred, ten hundred, how long has it been here? You ought to know—you're at one of these new-fangled schools where they turn out blue-stockinged young women."

"I'm sure I don't know, Papa," said Harriet happily.

"Oh, Harriet, Harriet," said her mother, looking up from her book. "And I thought history was your favorite subject. Well, I can only hope that your school report will give us better news—

you would have us believe that you are a terrible dunce, you know."

Harriet became silent at this. Not by the greatest stretch of the imagination could she hope that her report would be good. Every single one of her exercises always came back so heavily scarred with red ink that it was difficult to see where her own writing was.

But in this wonderful spring weather she could not remain depressed for long. She woke early next morning because of the sun that poured into her bedroom, and lay there thinking about how lovely the college garden had been, and wondering whether she could persuade Miss Edale to take her there. And from that she began turning over in her mind what that boy had told her about the Smiths. She remembered now what Mrs. Smith had said his name was: Luke Plover. He had given such a completely different picture of them from the one she had made for herself; it was hard to believe they had been talking about the same people. She thought back over the different times she had met them, and then she remembered the first time, when she had seen them at the Ashmolean Museum, and had so wanted to know them. It came as a shock, this memory—so she had liked them once. She screwed up her forehead, and tried to think of them as they seemed then. Thomas had been very knowledgeable and witty; Joshua had been the sort of person who was sorry for everything, even an old violin; and even James, the terrible James, had been no worse than rather a plague of a small brother. "Perhaps they think that I'm being as awful to them as I think they're being awful to me. But then I've never been so rude to them as they have to me. But perhaps if there were three of me, I might. And perhaps Jumbo *is* rather stupid." But as she said this, she was shocked at her disloyalty.

"Papa," she said, catching up with him after breakfast. "Do

you think it is a bad thing—this Jumbo League? Really, seriously," she added, afraid that he would tease as he usually did.

"You want my serious, considered opinion?" he said solemnly, halfway into his coat. "Well, I think it is the most
frightful nonsense, and in my opinion the whole English nation
has gone clean off its head—except your mother and myself."

"And Professor Smith, Papa," Harriet said ruefully.

"Oh, Professor Smith, if you like. Though poor old Fairy
wouldn't have it, eh Fairy? There's one thing though: I'll wager
that your Aunt Louisa doesn't get her army to London in time.
From what they say in the papers it looks as though they're
ready to ship old Jumbo off any minute now, and poor Louisa is
the most unpunctual woman alive. Now if it had been your
mother, she'd have had that army there weeks ago, and they'd
have done what they set out to do into the bargain. But your
mother, thank heaven, is more sensible. Tell you what, Hetty,"
he said suddenly. "We'll go to the cathedral on Sunday for the
morning service so that you can hear the singing. It's very fine
there, so they say, and it's a pity you shouldn't ever hear a good
choir."

"Oh, and then I can see where Miss Edale's altar cloth will
go," said Harriet, delighted.

So on Sunday, Harriet and her parents walked down into
Oxford to the cathedral. You had to approach it through the
huge quadrangle of the college of Christ Church, for though it
was the cathedral, it was also the college chapel. The quadrangle had its own charms; in the sunken garden in the middle,
surrounded by terraces, there was a fountain and a pool with
goldfish in it. But there was not much time to linger around
this, and they followed the hurrying undergraduates, who struggled into surplices as they strode over the gravel, into the
dimness of the cathedral, where the clangor of the bells sounded
muffled and far off. A few minutes later the procession of choir
and clergy moved slowly up the nave.

"There's old Canon Satisthwaite," said Dr. Jessop in a loud whisper to Harriet, pointing through the wrought-iron screen that separated the nave of the cathedral, where members of the college sat, from the seats of the rest of the congregation in the side aisles. "Patient of mine. He's going to preach today." At the tail of the procession Harriet saw the canon, a little old man with white hair shuffling along some way behind the other clergy.

In the end it was Canon Satisthwaite's sermon, and not the hymn in Latin or the beautiful singing of the choir, that made the service so memorable. It was all about Jumbo. It took Harriet a long time to realize this because he spoke rather indistinctly and swallowed a lot, and besides, he never referred to Jumbo by name, he always called him "our noble beast" and said he was an ancient symbol of something or other. He did not even refer to the "noble beast" until about the middle of the sermon; he spent a long time describing how the Romans baited animals and made spectacles of them, and said look what had happened to the Roman civilization. Was this to happen to the English civilization? And then he began on the cruel inhumanity of allowing the "noble beast" to leave English shores to go to a nation of slave owners. Harriet could hardly believe she heard aright. To talk about an elephant in a sermon! She looked sideways at her father; he was shaking his head and tapping his foot impatiently.

"Papa," she breathed in his ear at last. "Is it about *Jumbo?*"

"It is indeed," he said, rather loudly.

The congregation seemed to have grasped this at about the same time, for there was a flutter and rustle through the long lines of chairs in the side aisles, and in the nave where the members of the college sat, young men in surplices turned to each other and murmured. None of this disturbed old Canon Satisthwaite. He went on in his quavering voice, never lifting his eyes from his notes which he turned over with hands encased in purple mittens.

Under the cover of the hymn that followed the sermon there must have been a great deal of comment going on, Harriet thought, but most of it had to be reserved for when the congregation poured out into the sun through the porch of the great west door. Then there was a sound like the chattering of thousands of starlings. Harriet began to question her father eagerly, but he was looking in the opposite direction, and bowing.

"Friends of yours," he said.

Through the groups of bare-headed undergraduates came the Smith family in procession, Professor Smith in a silk hat and Mrs. Smith in purple followed by four boys.

"Things have come to a pretty pass when we get all this nonsense about an elephant from the pulpit," Dr. Jessop called out suddenly to the professor in a voice loud enough to make several people turn around.

The professor raised his hat, and came over. Harriet anxiously watched his face, wondering if he was going to be terribly angry and start talking about Aunt Louisa. But he really looked quite genial. "Scandalous thing," he said. "I've never known anything like it all the years I've been in the University. Satisthwaite must be out of his mind. Well, he'll have an uneasy Sunday of it with all Christ Church about his ears."

"He won't care tuppence," said Dr. Jessop sorrowfully. "He's as deaf as a post. That ear trumpet affair of his—thing that looks like a silver vegetable dish—is just for an ornament. No use at all. But nothing that I can say will make him change it."

"No doubt he uses it to tease the people who speak to him," said the professor, who seemed in a high good humor now. Harriet looked for the first time at the boys, whose eyes she had been nervously avoiding. They did not look nearly so man-eating today, and they were actually listening to her father.

Joshua even gave rather a timid smile in her direction. Perhaps, thought Harriet, with a lightening of her heart, Luke Plover has told them that it was all a mistake about Papa and the dog. Only James stood rather crossly apart. Luke edged up to her.

"Did you hear that noise when the sermon was going on? It was James, he kept on saying, 'It *is* Jumbo he's talking about, isn't it? Well, why doesn't he say so.' He kept on and on—you know how he does. And I was next to him, too. Uncle Alfred was very angry."

James came over to them now. "I know Papa isn't going to give me my Saturday penny. Luke, can you lend me one, Mrs. Juke's got twenty aniseed balls for a ha'penny—it's special because it's the bottom of the bottle, and they'll all be gone by next week. Oh, Luke, do; Joshua says he won't and it's no good asking Thomas."

"Don't you," said Thomas from a distance. "Nor you either," he added to Harriet, who was so overpowered at being spoken to by Thomas and not shouted at that she blushed.

"Well," said Dr. Jessop as they walked back to North Oxford over the sunny pavements. "Any little bit of feeling there might have been between Professor Smith and myself has vanished over Canon Satisthwaite's sermon—we are both of the same mind about it, it seems. And what are your own feelings about Jumbo, Hetty? You still as much for him as ever you were?"

"I don't know, Papa." Harriet felt in a thorough muddle about the whole thing. "It seems very peculiar to put him into a sermon, and I suppose some of the things that people do are rather silly, but all the same, I do wish he wouldn't go to America."

"Well said, Hetty, there's hope for you yet. Last week you wanted to kill anybody who disagreed; now you're not so sure. Did you say there was a wing rib of beef, Alice? Well then, we'd better hasten our steps, I think. Roll on, the wing rib, that's what I say."

But at school on Monday the Oxford Ladies had not lost an ounce of enthusiasm for Jumbo. "There was a sermon about him in the cathedral," said Agatha very importantly.

"I know," Harriet told her. "I was there. But I don't think they ought to put elephants into sermons."

Agatha opened her eyes wide. "Oh, Harriet, you're not going to give up Jumbo, are you? Why, you were the one who started it. And we're having another drill today, and your aunt is going to tell us the day that we're going to march."

Harriet did not know what to say. She was in two minds about it, not wanting to be a deserter, but remembering what her father and what Luke Plover had said. "You'll never be able to march to London," she said at last. "I know a boy and he said that when he walked for ten miles he was terribly tired. And London's much farther than that."

"But of course we're not walking; how silly you are," said Agatha impatiently. "There's a special train. There'll be people from Birmingham and I don't know where on it. It will be very inspiring," she added primly. "And then we'll march from Paddington to the London Zoological Gardens—with my banner."

"And what are we going to do when we get there?" said Harriet, remembering all Luke's arguments.

"I expect we'll demonstrate," said Agatha vaguely. "Your aunt hasn't told us about that yet."

"Well, Papa says unless you hurry, Jumbo will be in America before you get to London. They're making his crate now for him to travel in."

Agatha looked at her accusingly. "Harriet, you speak as though you were a traitor."

"I don't see why you should say I'm a traitor just because I want to know what you're going to do," said Harriet angrily. She spent most of the rest of the day wondering whether she would or would not join in the drill. She was still undecided when she went slowly out of school at the end of the afternoon, buttoning up her coat as she walked. A shout from the playground made her jump.

"Come along there, come along there, fall in. We can't wait here all night," bellowed a raucous voice. Harriet saw most of the girls already lined up in front of the sergeant and looking over their shoulders at her rather smugly. Covered with confusion, she hurried to take her place.

" 'Shun!" roared the sergeant, and the rather crooked line shuffled its feet together. "Right about . . . turn. Forward . . . march. Come along, come along, have a bit of spirit. Think of trooping the color, marching to fight the h'enemy. Marching to save your blooming h'elephant, if you like, but look alive. Alive, I said!" he roared even louder. "Not like potted shrimps."

Through the shuffle of marching feet and the bellowing of the sergeant there suddenly came the voice of the second mistress. It took everybody by surprise, and they all turned and stared.

"Now then, now then," rasped the sergeant. "Just what do you think you're adoing of? That's mutiny, that is. When you're on parade you're under orders—d'ye see. Now, eyes front, and keep them front—even if the Day of Judgment comes while you've got them there."

"One minute, Sergeant, if you please," called the second mistress. The parade straggled to a halt and stood and gazed at her as she stood on the steps outside the door. They really could not help it, they were more used to taking orders from the second mistress than from a sergeant.

"There is a small boy here who came and asked for Miss Raby." The second mistress looked behind her and beckoned somebody forward. "He says if he can't see Miss Raby he wants to see somebody called Harriet or Agatha. Come here, little boy."

Below her, in the playground, the parade of girls tittered. The second mistress pushed forward a small red-headed boy; James, of course. Harriet remembered her parting words to him in Longwall Street on Friday, and felt quite sick. Agatha, next to her, was even more stricken.

"It's that awful boy who shouts things at us. How ever did he get here? How does he know my name *and* yours?"

"Perhaps Aunt Louisa told him." Harriet eyed James nervously, and thought it would be stupid to tell Agatha now just how mixed up with James she had been.

Agatha made an exasperated noise. "Well, she shouldn't have. She must know how awful he is. Oh, but she would do anything. She even broke an umbrella hitting a cabman."

All this chatter could hardly escape the sergeant. He made a ferocious growling noise in his throat. "Did I hear *talking* there in the ranks?" He marched up to them at a furious rate. Agatha and Harriet quailed, and stepped back a couple of paces, almost afraid that they would be bayoneted by those pointed mustaches. It was quite impossible now to remember the sergeant as the mild man who had apologized at the end of the first drill.

"Sergeant," called the second mistress in a voice that sounded light and fluting after his throaty growl, "This little boy seems to want to do some drill too. Perh⋯ ⋯ld take him over. Run along, little boy."

James clambered down the step⋯ hand a jar with a string tied arour⋯ my tadpoles where none of the⋯ he demanded.

Again there was smothered⋯ however, was not at all am⋯ "How dare he? How dare⋯ breath, but only loud en⋯ just watched him with⋯

a loss for words. "Well, you are a rum little perisher and no mistake," he said at last.

James was not in the least put out by any of this. It was doubtful whether he even noticed. He surveyed the playground carefully. "Well, I'll put them here," he said, placing the jar on the bottom step. "But if anybody knocks them over I'll hit them."

"Oh, I'd like to hit *him*," said Agatha between her teeth.

"Now what shall I do?" remarked James, looking at the parade. "They're not in a very straight line. Fancy girls drilling. I bet they can't do it properly." He attached himself to the end of the front line, and stood at ease, his legs wide apart, his arms behind his back, eyeing the sergeant watchfully.

The sergeant pulled himself together. "Parade, 'shun!" he roared. "Forward march."

Everybody marched except James, who was left standing there. "Why didn't you say 'Shoulder hipe'?" he demanded.

"Because young ladies don't carry rifles, that's why, and gawd help us if they did, this lot," said the sergeant, looking at the straggling parade and shaking his head despairingly.

James stood where he was and watched too. "Shall I carry the flag?" he said. "That girl doesn't know how to carry it. I know, I've seen it in pictures."

"Well, you couldn't do it much worse, I suppose," said the sergeant gloomily, watching Agatha stumbling over the stick and pushing the flapping folds of the flag out of her eyes. "But carrying pictures of elephants around, I ask you!"

He halted the parade and commanded the color party to take ⌐e forward. Agatha, who had heard all the exchanges ⌐mes and the sergeant, did so, her hands trembling ⌐n the sergeant ordered her to hand the banner ⌐most afraid she would try to ram James with ⌐ sergeant and his bristling mustaches kept her silent, and she merely pushed it into his arms with such force that he staggered back. So when the parade moved off again James strutted proudly in front, holding the banner well up, with one hand clutching the free end to the pole so that it could not flap. Around and around they went, and Harriet was just beginning to feel again what an inspiring thing it was to march, when a high and quavering voice said "Halt."

A few girls did halt, but the rest, remembering what had been said last time about going on no matter what happened, went on marching, though they were bold enough to look and see who it was. It was Aunt Louisa, wild-eyed, distraught, a newspaper in her hand. Harriet's immediate thought was that something must have happened to her parents, some dreadful accident, and she too stopped, and gazed at her aunt.

"Halt, I said. Sergeant, stop them. It is all over, the knell has sounded."

Harriet, desperate by now, was about to break ranks and rush up to her aunt to find out what had happened. But her aunt, seeing that the girls were already standing there gazing, held up her hand. "Jumbo goes tomorrow. Our efforts have been in vain. Disperse." And she turned on her heel and walked away.

The girls stood there, staring after her. The sergeant took off his pillbox hat and stared too, muttering, "Well, I'll be blowed." But Harriet felt an enormous wave of relief that it was only bad news about an elephant.

"Does she mean that we're not going to march to London, after all?" James's penetrating voice demanded. "Does she?" he said even louder, looking around at everybody. "Well, does she?"

"Didn't you hear?" said Agatha furiously. "He's going to America tomorrow. Why can't you listen instead of talking so much?"

James hurled down the banner. "Well, why didn't we go

before? I kept saying why didn't we, and nobody did anything. And we won't be able to, ever, and I won't be able to have a ride on Jumbo." There were tears of anger in his eyes. "It's all your fault," he raged, turning on Agatha and Harriet, and trampling on the banner. "You never did anything when I told you."

"Get off my flag." Agatha advanced on James with such a look of fury that Harriet thought she must be going to attack him, and hastily stepped forward.

"Take your silly old flag," said James contemptuously, removing his foot. "It doesn't look much like an elephant, and why's it got that red thing on its back? Jumbo didn't."

"You're the most hateful boy that ever lived," said Agatha, bending down to pick up her flag. "And the stupidest."

Harriet grabbed him by the shoulder, feeling that not a moment must be lost in removing him from the school premises. Otherwise anything might happen; Agatha might attack him, or, worst of all horrors, Miss Raby herself might return. She had half dared him to come—though she had never meant it that way—and she must now take him away.

"Come on," she said. "And hurry up." Through the railings she could see the large pale face of Miss Edale peering at her anxiously, and felt rather guilty that she had again kept her waiting.

"I suppose I might as well. Anyway, it's silly marching with a lot of girls." James gave a final disconsolate kick to the flag as it trailed on the ground. "The parade hasn't been dismissed yet, though."

Harriet gave the sergeant a furtive look. He was scratching his head in a puzzled way, and had his hat under his arm. "Rum do," Harriet heard him say. "Rummiest do *I* ever came across." He seemed to have turned safely into a mild family man again, and she judged it would be all right to go.

Miss Edale met them outside. "Your poor aunt," she said.

"She seemed very upset about the elephant. Still, it is all no doubt for the best." Then she looked at James with consternation. "Dear me, is this little boy with us again?"

"I'm going to see your aunt," announced James loudly. "I'm going to ask her why I can't go to London and fight them. Girls aren't any good. But I bet I could make them listen to me."

"Oh no you're not," said Harriet. "You're going home this minute." She supposed that in a way it was partly her fault that he was here at all, and she was not going to have him doing any more damage. "Do your brothers and people know where you are?"

"I ran away from them," said James triumphantly. "We were doing a boring natural history walk with Mr. Ledgard, and I just ran away."

"Your poor mama," said Miss Edale, scandalized. "She will be nearly beside herself."

"You've got to go back, straight away," commanded Harriet. "You ran away before, and your brothers said I had made you."

"Yes, they did," said James indifferently. "They were frightfully angry."

"You're a very wicked boy." Harriet was infuriated by his calmness. "And they're not going to say that now because we're going to take you back, aren't we, Miss Edale?"

"I certainly think we should, Harriet," said Miss Edale, who had a strong sense of duty. "His poor mama will be distracted."

So they marched down into Oxford with James, sulky and morose, in the middle of them, like a prisoner escorted by two policemen. Harriet kept giving him nervous little glances, wondering what they would do if he just took it into his head to bolt. But James, however awful, seemed to have some respect for authority. Not a word was said. Miss Edale was probably sorrowing over the lost time which might have been spent on her lace, and Harriet was far too anxious in case James should escape.

It seemed a very long way, but at last they turned the corner into Canterbury Lane. "Oh, there they are," said James casually. And at the bottom of the street Harriet could see Thomas and Joshua. They came running toward James and his escort. But Harriet was determined that on this occasion she was going to get her version in first. She was not going to let them accuse her of stealing away their brother and then refuse to listen when she tried to explain.

"We've brought James back!" she said while they were still quite twenty yards away. But she could wait no longer; she felt foolish marching toward them wondering what expression to wear. "He said he'd run away from you so we thought we had better bring him all the way back in case he ran away again."

"James, how could you!" Joshua said to him. "We've been all over the parks looking for you, and Mama's in such a terrible state again—Mr. Ledgard's with her now trying to calm her down."

"Mr. Ledgard's natural history walks are so stupid," said James sulkily. "Besides, I wanted to practice for the march to London, but now there isn't going to be one."

Thomas turned to Harriet. "Thank you for bringing him back. I expect he's been a frightful nuisance—he always is." He spoke in an offhand way, but Harriet felt quite a glow of pleasure.

Joshua left Thomas to carry on scolding James, and came over to Harriet. He frowned at his boots in a nervous way. "I'm sorry about what we said to you once about your father bringing a dog into Mama's room when she was ill. Luke asked Papa about it the other day, and Papa said that the dog followed him in and that it was all a mistake."

Harriet thought it was nice of Joshua, but she still could not understand how the mistake had been made. "But I told you and told you," she said plaintively. "So did Papa."

Joshua shuffled uneasily. "I suppose you did, but we were so angry about it that we didn't seem to take it in."

Miss Edale, who was always uneasy in Canterbury Lane, feeling that somebody from the needlework shop would pounce upon her and drag her in and force her to make purchases, put an end to further conversation.

"Harriet, we must go. We are already late," she said, looking uneasily over her shoulder.

They were halfway up Canterbury Lane when a roar from James reached their ears. "Those girls have got my tadpoles. Tell them to bring them back."

Chapter 14

Tadpoles in Canterbury Lane

"*B*ut where's your black armband?" said Agatha when Harriet arrived at school the next morning. "You've got to have one."

"Who said?" Harriet looked around the playground in a bewildered way. Certainly it was peppered with black armbands; some of the girls had even gone to the length of wearing widows' caps, in which they looked extremely self-conscious.

"Your aunt said yesterday that we ought to do it out of respect for Jumbo. You had gone off early, as usual. I don't know what's come over you nowadays. Never mind though, you can make an armband out of the blackboard duster in our classroom. You can put it back after prayers."

"No, I don't think I will," said Harriet uneasily.

"Why? Nobody will know it's a duster if you brush it a bit."

"Well, it does seem rather silly." Harriet chewed the finger of her glove unhappily. "I mean, it's not doing Jumbo any good if I put the blackboard duster around my arm."

"Oh, Harriet, how could you? You used to be so keen, and

now you're just a traitor. It's the last thing you can do for Jumbo, and now you won't do it."

"But what good is it?" Harriet always got more determined if anybody argued with her. "And I think those girls in caps look silly."

All the same, she did feel conspicuous when they marched into prayers. She screwed her head around in all directions, trying to find somebody else who was not wearing black. Some of the older girls were without armbands, but then they wore mourning brooches or some sort of jet ornament. Nevertheless they did all look a little self-conscious as they filed through the open door of the assembly hall. The second mistress was a mild woman, but would even she let this pass without comment? So there was a great deal of grimacing over shoulders, and shrugging, and raised eyebrows in the passage outside. The girls in the widows' caps especially pulled them this way and that, and carried their heads at an uneasy angle until they were inside the assembly hall. Once there they stood frozen, as if by their stillness they could distract attention from themselves. For on the dais, with a grim expression on her face and her eyes like granite, stood Miss Raby.

Nothing was said until prayers were over. The Oxford Ladies sang the hymn with great fervor, some of them hoping that if they sang it superlatively well Miss Raby would be moved to overlook everything. But she was not. As soon as the lesson for the day and the prayers had been read, she told them in a quiet, grim voice just how childish and foolish they were, how unfit to become responsible adults, how unfit even to be outside the nursery. She saw no possible future for any of them—even marriage—and certainly none as the responsible leaders of their sex that she hoped they would be. A lot of the girls wept as she spoke on and on in this vein. Finally, she ordered everybody who was taking part in this absurd charade to come forward and place whatever ludicrous gewgaw she was wearing on the dais in front of her. She proposed to have them put in a glass case as a perpetual memory to others of the supreme folly of this present generation of the Oxford Ladies' College. At first nobody moved. They stood there dazed and not sure whether the order was not just more sarcasm. But Miss Raby ordered them again, in sharper tones, asking whether they were deaf, or just disobedient. At that, a miserable small girl in the bottom form, standing in front, crept forward with her black armband, and arranged it very neatly in exactly the middle of the dais, at Miss Raby's feet. She was followed by the rest of her form. And slowly the whole school filed after them, standing in long lines before Miss Raby, waiting to add their contribution to the black pile. Only Harriet was left, very conspicuous and very embarrassed, in the middle of the hall. She wished that she had joined her class and pretended to have something to put on the pile, but now it was too late, and she had to stand there feeling horribly alone and unprotected and silly, for Miss Raby and all the mistresses behind her to stare at and mark down.

At last it came to an end, and they all somberly filed out to their various classrooms, where they sat, very subdued and still, through the morning's lessons. Harriet felt like an outcast, and avoided everybody at break. But when the school dispersed for luncheon, Agatha cornered her in the cloakroom.

"You did look silly," she said, "standing there all by yourself."

"I couldn't help it," Harriet said miserably.

"It was all because you rushed away so early yesterday. Otherwise you would have heard us all saying that we were going to wear mourning." This was hardly fair. But Harriet did not argue. "What *were* you doing, anyway?" Agatha went on.

"I took James Smith back to his home," said Harriet with spirit, "so that he couldn't be a nuisance any more."

"James Smith!" Agatha spoke the name with deep loathing. "How did he know to come, anyway? Asking for Miss Raby or

Harriet or Agatha. Harriet, did you tell him that we were doing drill?"

Harriet could only nod guiltily. "Well, really," Agatha went on, "I'd thought you would have more sense. How could you, when you know how awful he is. I just hope we've seen the last of him anyway, or I don't know what I'll do to him."

"I don't think we have seen the last of him. He says he left his tadpoles here and he wants them back." As soon as she had said this Harriet knew what a terrible mistake it was. She should have let the matter rest, instead of enraging Agatha still more. But she would never have guessed just how angry it would make Agatha. Every muscle in her face went stiff with rage, and when she spoke it was through her teeth.

"He wants them back, does he. Well, he will have them back. I'll just show him how horrible he is and how horrible his tadpoles are."

She grabbed her coat and her hat, and flew out of the cloakroom. The passage door slammed behind her with such violence that it sounded as though the glass panes would break. Harriet was left standing there in great agitation, wondering what fearful thing Agatha would do in her rage. She was gone for the whole of luncheon; nobody knew of it, except Harriet, who watched the doors of the dining room uneasily, and, after the meal was over, went outside to peer through the railings, waiting for her to come back. When the bell rang for afternoon school, she was still not back, but just before the first class began she slid into her place, red-faced and panting, but all the same looking pleased with herself.

"Where have you been?" Harriet said to her urgently.

"I've been to take back the tadpoles."

"Whatever do you mean?" said Harriet, stricken.

"I've poured them in through the letter box on his front door. You know, the one marked Canterbury College Lodgings."

Harriet sat down in her seat with a bang and looked at

Agatha, with a stricken face. "You didn't. Not through the Lodgings door?"

"Yes I did. I opened the letter box and I emptied the jar through. Some of the tadpoles went on the doorstep, but not many." Agatha's face had a smile of triumph.

"You put them through the door with 'Lodgings' on it?" insisted Harriet again.

Agatha was impatient. "Yes, I keep telling you."

"Well, that's not James Smith's front door. It belongs to the Warden of Canterbury College."

How Agatha took this Harriet did not notice; she was far too overwhelmed with the frightful thing that had been done. It would have been bad enough if it had been the Smiths' front door, but the Lodgings! Harriet remembered the snowy whiteness of the step on that occasion when Professor Smith had told her whom the house belonged to, and she thought of the tadpoles now sprawling all over it. All through the afternoon's classes she sat in a daze, paying no heed to the lessons, and not even listening when the mistresses called her to attention. It was really all her fault, through and through. She had begun the Jumbo excitement; she had infected Agatha; she had told James to come to the school, and then had maddened Agatha by telling her what he had said. Only in the final five minutes of the last lesson of the afternoon did she become aware of what was going on around her. This was when a small girl from the very bottom form of the school came in and laid something on the teacher's desk. Miss Robbins examined it, and then called out Harriet's name. She did not hear it at once, but her neighbors did, and prodded her awake. Harriet stumbled out and was given a letter addressed to her father in Miss Raby's handwriting. So Miss Raby knew it all too, and this was how she was setting about expelling her.

"We must go home straight away," she said wildly to Miss Edale outside the gate as she came out of school, and she set off at a furious pace. Miss Edale, bewildered and agitated, was hard put to it to keep up, and several times Harriet, hearing a faint and breathless voice behind her calling her to go more slowly, had to stand and wait for her to catch up.

At last they were back, and Harriet burst into the study, almost without knocking. Dr. Jessop was sleeping in his deep leather armchair, a silk handkerchief over his eyes, and Fairy snoring on the hearth rug beside him. He grunted and pulled the handkerchief away.

"Papa," said Harriet sobbingly, "I've been expelled. Miss Raby has written to say so. And Papa, it's much worse than that. Because of what I said to one of the girls, she went and poured tadpoles through the front door of the Lodgings of Canterbury College."

Dr. Jessop looked sleepy and bewildered. "But what have you been up to that they've got to expel you?"

Fairy stretched herself and came and sniffed in a friendly way around Harriet's legs, but she brushed her impatiently away. "It's because of what I said to Agatha, and telling James Smith to come to the school," said Harriet incoherently.

"But I don't see how anything you said to James Smith and this Agatha could be bad enough for them to expel you."

"But such dreadful things happened because of what I said." Harriet was sobbing by now. "I mean putting tadpoles through the front door, and it was the wrong front door too." She was in such distress that she did not notice that the door had opened and her mother had come in.

"Why, Harriet," she said, "whatever is wrong? And what are you doing home so early?"

"There's some story about being expelled and tadpoles and the wrong front door," said Dr. Jessop. "But Hetty, you'll have to explain more than that."

So gaspingly and not very clearly she poured out the story about Jumbo and Agatha and James. "And Papa, I'll have to go and tell them at the Lodgings that it was all my fault and say I'm sorry." She thought again of those tadpoles wriggling on the beautiful step, and shuddered. "Now. I *must*."

To her enormous surprise, her mother, who had said nothing all through her rambling story, came over and kissed her, which was something she very rarely did. "Harriet," she said, "you have more courage and sense of responsibility than I ever suspected. If you go now I am sure your father will take you down."

"Will you, Papa?" asked Harriet, who had expected no more than the rather doubtful support of Miss Edale.

"Certainly, Hetty, my dear. We can't have you braving unknown university gentlemen by yourself." He heaved himself out of his chair. "We'll drive down. I told them to have the gig ready by about this time."

But though to drive with her father was usually a great pleasure, Harriet was brooding too much on the terrors that lay ahead even to notice it.

"Want me to come in with you?" Dr. Jessop asked as they drew up outside the Lodgings. Harriet shook her head. "Cheer up, then," he said. "It'll soon be over." And as she stood drooping there on the doorstep waiting for them to answer the bell, he called to her again: "Ten minutes at the most, and it'll all be over."

But ten minutes can be a very long time. Even the wait for the door to be opened was like a whole afternoon at school. She looked nervously at the steps; they had been newly washed and were not yet dry—it spoke for itself; so did the empty jam jar with the piece of string tied around it which was lying in the gutter.

Steps came down the hall within, and Harriet braced back her shoulders and clenched her fists. "I want to see the warden, please," she said to the parlormaid.

"Well, I don't know that he's at home, miss," said the maid very doubtfully, looking her up and down.

"But I must," she said urgently. "It's terribly important." She hesitated. "It's about those tadpoles."

"That nasty horrid mess all over the hall?" said the maid indignantly. "Well, you ought to be ashamed of yourself, miss, that's all I can say. But you can't go bothering the warden with the likes of that. He's a very busy gentleman. You'd better see Mrs. Clomper the housekeeper instead. She'll soon tell you what she thinks of you."

"But I must see him," said Harriet desperately. "It wasn't me that did it, but I want to explain."

"Hallo, hallo, hallo, what's all the trouble?" said a voice at her shoulder. But it was not her father. It was Professor Smith, just about the last person she could possibly have wished to see.

"Haven't you come to the wrong door?" He smiled at her benevolently. "Is it one of my boys you're after?"

"I wanted to see the Warden of Canterbury College," said Harriet, thoroughly flustered and ill at ease.

"Then you are at the right door, and as I myself am going to see the warden you can come with me." He waved aside the parlormaid, who seemed to know him well, and pushing Harriet ahead of him, he marched down the long hall, dark with paneling, and peopled with portraits of past wardens. A grandfather clock ticked loudly; otherwise it was the stillest house Harriet had ever been in. Professor Smith knocked loudly on a door at the far end, and hardly waiting for an answer, threw it open.

Harriet found herself in a room that was all she could ever have imagined an Oxford scholar's study would be like. It was dark, lined from floor to ceiling with row upon row of books, and it had a smell rather like a church. A tall, stooping man rose from a desk near the window.

"Good afternoon, Warden," said Professor Smith briskly. "This young lady is determined to see you. Her name, I think, is Miss Jessop, Miss Harriet Jessop, perhaps we should say, to distinguish her from her aunt—who is a lady of great strength of character who has done me the compliment of joining battle with me."

The warden pulled at his hooked nose, and looked at Harriet in a puzzled way. Harriet looked back, licking her dry lips, and wondering feverishly where in this long, long story she ought to start. He was such a clever man, and probably so very busy that she ought to keep her story short and clear, and not waste his time. She swallowed and began.

"It was because of my aunt. She got interested in Jumbo— the elephant, you know—and I got interested too, and then everybody at the Oxford Ladies' College did and Agatha most of all. Then Agatha got so cross with James Smith for coming and drilling with us for our march to London, and for leaving his tadpoles at school that she took them and poured them through the letter box. Only it was the wrong letter box, it was the Lodgings. I mean, she shouldn't have poured them at all, but it was worse being the wrong house. And they must have made a horrid mess—the maid said they did—and really I'm so awfully sorry."

"I might have known that James was mixed up in it somewhere," said Professor Smith cheerfully. "But the audacity of him leaving his tadpoles at the Oxford Ladies' College! I shall have to write a letter of apology to the formidable Miss Raby."

But the warden still looked at Harriet in a puzzled way. "But my dear young lady, it does not seem to be at all your fault that this misfortune happened."

"Oh, but it was," she burst out. "If it hadn't been for me, Agatha would never have got interested, and I kept telling her that she ought to get more. And I sort of dared James to come to the school—though I didn't mean to—and it made her furious, and then she got furiouser because I told her what

James had said about wanting his tadpoles back. And even then I could have taken the tadpoles away from her, but I didn't."

"Young lady, you have a conscience like my son Joshua's, I perceive," said the professor, patting her shoulder. "A good thing in this naughty world, I would say."

"A very good thing indeed," said the warden, smiling at last. "I completely accept your apologies, my dear Miss Jessop; the damage to the front doorstep is trivial, I am sure. Please do not worry about it."

And that was all. Harriet could hardly believe that the terror was over so soon and so easily. There was only the minor difficulty left of knowing how to take her leave, and wondering whether it was now the moment to do so. "I think I ought to go now," she said awkwardly. "Papa is waiting for me."

"Dr. Jessop," said Professor Smith by way of explanation to the warden. "My compliments to your father, young lady, and tell him I hope he will allow you to visit us sometimes. Perhaps my nephew Luke might accompany you on your walks. He is on holiday just now, and gets bored, I think, while the others are at their lessons."

Then the warden spoke. "I wonder," he said, "if they would spare you to visit the Lodgings after Easter. My great-niece, Maria, is to spend a few days with me on her way to school, and this is a dull house for a young girl. I should like her to have some company of her own age. It is April the twentieth that she arrives. Perhaps if you took tea with her on April the twenty-first . . ."

When Harriet climbed up beside her father into the gig, she was almost too overcome with emotion to speak. "Papa," she said in an awestricken way. "They've asked me to tea at the Lodgings, on April the twenty-first; the warden's going to write to Mama. It's to play with the warden's niece. And Professor Smith said could you spare me to go and see the boys one day." As she said this she remembered that afternoon in the museum

when she had first seen the boys and had desired nothing more
than to know them. And the times when she had walked
through the streets past the Oxford colleges, longing to know
the people who lived in them. And now she had been asked to
tea by the Warden of Canterbury College himself. She had
never in her whole life been happier than this.

"That's one hurdle successfully jumped," said her father cheerfully. "Now what about being expelled? We'll have to try to get
you over that one too."

A cold shiver went through Harriet. She had completely
forgotten. Dully she fumbled in her coat pocket and pulled out
the crumpled note in Miss Raby's handwriting. "Here is the
letter," she said in a flat voice. All the happiness and relief had
gone; she wondered how she had ever felt it.

Dr. Jessop took off a glove and tore open the envelope.
Harriet sat and stared straight ahead of her, not daring to watch
his face. Then her father gave a sudden shout of laughter and
clapped her on the back. "Now how ever did you get it into
your head that she was expelling you, Hetty? She is writing to
say that alone in the Oxford Ladies' College, in spite of all the
hysterical folly around you, you kept a proper sense of pro-
proportion. Great strength of character, she says, expects great
things of you, a credit to your parents. Well, well, Hetty, you're
a chip off the old block, all right. Your mother's block, that is
to say."

Harriet felt almost giddy. "Papa, are you sure it's right?
You're not joking, are you?"

Dr. Jessop was hurt. "Now as if I'd joke about a thing like
that. Here's the letter; you see for yourself."

Harriet took it feverishly. It was all there, just as her father
had said, written in Miss Raby's small, precise handwriting. She
could not believe it. There must be a mistake somewhere.

"Well, it's your mother's side you get it from, certainly not
from mine—look at poor Louisa—in fact she should have been

the person to go and apologize to the warden. We should never have allowed an impressionable young creature like you to go around with her. Might have known she'd start trying to recruit you to her wildcat causes."

"Poor Aunt Louisa," said Harriet. "What will she do without Jumbo?"

"Oh, haven't you heard the latest thing? She's championing the cause of the mouse that was badly frightened by being put into a python's cage. Anyway, she'll be triumphant when she sees this." He tapped the newspaper that lay on his knee. "They got Jumbo into his crate, it seems, but Jumbo had the last word; he tweaked the tails of the horses who were pulling the cart and they bolted. Good old Jumbo, sagacious beast." Dr. Jessop roared with laughter.

"Which will she feel sorry for," Harriet asked doubtfully. "Jumbo or the horses?"

He gave another roar of laughter. "Well done, Hetty, well done. Which indeed? It'll give her something to think about all right. Now look, here's Thrupp and Drabble. How about buying a dress to make up for the one that was too small? A pretty dress. You're a pretty little thing, and you'll make a good wife someday. So don't go bothering so much about what happens at school. It really doesn't matter. Your school days are soon over. And keep off causes too. Your mother and your aunt are quite enough for one man."

"Oh, Papa," said Harriet, whose mind was only on the dress. "And can I wear it when I go to tea with the warden's niece?"

And that night she took her list of battles, and wrote right across the page in careful capitals: "ELEPHANT WAR FIN- ISHED APRIL, 1875," and she buried it at the bottom of the garden.

Afterword

Jean Fritz

From the moment I met her, I knew that Harriet was my kind of heroine. There she is in a museum in Oxford, England, pretending to look at a display of Greek coins while in fact she is eavesdropping on three brothers who are making interesting and witty remarks about an old violin in the next case. One of the boys even feels sorry for the violin stuck behind the glass, unable either to hear or make music. I too want to know these boys, so I'm with Harriet all the way as she tries to track them down. It doesn't take her long to find out that they are the sons of a Professor Smith, but I'm pretty pessimistic about what will happen next. Knowing the way authors operate, I can guess that Harriet will have to make enemies with the boys before she can make friends.

It's really the fault of the grown-ups. Everyone knows how embarrassing grown-ups can be in the most ordinary circum-stances, but why does Harriet's father have to get things off to such a bad start when Harriet first meets the Smiths? Why does he have to make such a big deal about the pedigree of his

Dalmatian dog who accompanies him everywhere? He informs the Smiths (and everyone else within hearing) whom the dog is "out of," right down to the fact that the dog's father was "sired by Fallowfield Ferox himself."

I groan. Of course the Smith boys find this hilarious, and from that time on they call Harriet "Fallowfield Ferox" or witty variations thereof. The war is on. I like the fact that Harriet keeps track of the battles, her victories and her losses; and I suffer with her through her many embarrassments. It is not surprising that her family, being the sort of grown-ups that they are, make things worse. All the adult women in this book are the pits, and I hate it when Harriet feels guilty about not being more like her mother. Fortunately, I don't think there's a chance that she will turn out that way. But Aunt Louisa! She's the one who is really off the wall. At the moment she is up to her ears in a campaign to keep Jumbo, the elephant at the London Zoo, from being sold to Mr. Barnum of America.

All over England people are upset about Jumbo, and I can understand that Harriet, who once fed buns to the elephant, would be too. But she makes a big mistake when she gets caught up in her aunt's campaign. It's hard for the reader to care about an elephant who never even sticks his trunk into the story, and we do wish Harriet would get off the Jumbo kick. It's too much—all that business of stuffing letter boxes with "Save Jumbo" pamphlets! All the silly talk of Jumbo going to a nation of savage barbarians who own slaves! Aunt Louisa conveniently overlooks the fact that the only time Jumbo was free was in his native country, Abyssinia, before he was captured. Moreover, Aunt Louisa doesn't have American history straight. This is 1875, and slaves in America were freed on January 1, 1863. But Aunt Louisa is invincible. She even arranges for a sergeant to drill the girls in Harriet's school in preparation for a march on London.

We have to be patient because we do like Harriet and know

that eventually she'll come to her senses. And she does. She ends up friends with the Smith boys too, just as I knew she would.

Meanwhile I became so fed up with Jumbo, I decided to find out his real story. And do you know that when it came time for Mr. Barnum's agent to load Jumbo into his cage to go to America, Jumbo lay down on a London street and refused to budge? The agent cabled Mr. Barnum. "What shall I do?" he asked. "Let him lie," Mr. Barnum cabled back. "It's the best advertisement in the world." To think that Aunt Louisa missed a scene like that!

And I wonder why the author didn't tell us that Jumbo was the largest elephant the civilized world had ever seen—ten feet, ten inches tall, weighing eight tons. What's more, it wasn't so bad in America, after all. Jumbo traveled in a special "palace" car of the circus train and made great friends with a baby elephant named Tom Thumb. Of course Jumbo did come to a rather abrupt end. Standing on a railroad track in Canada, he was hit and killed by a train.

In any case, it's Harriet that I'm interested in. I like to think of her running around Oxford with the Smith boys, exchanging witty remarks. In a dull moment she may take time out for her favorite daydream. She likes to think that some day she'll wake up beautiful, speaking French perfectly. I can go along with a dream like that.